THE WOLF OF DORIAN GRAY

A Werewolf Spawned by the Evil of Man

BRIAN S. FERENCE

ISBN-13: 978-0998325200 (Brian S. Ference)
ISBN-10: 0998325201

Dedication

My thanks go out to my beautiful wife Rachel, the love of my life, who supports me in everything that I do. I wrote this book as an experiment, an exercise in thought, a journey of imagination, and an exploration of conscious. I have long held a fascination with werewolves and have always had the goal to publish a book. Enjoy this compelling tale of love, lust, and the werewolf spawned by the evil of man.

TABLE OF CONTENTS

I

PROLOGUE

James approached the crumbling stone wall of the vast country estate. He'd have to move quickly to avoid detection from the other men tramping through the dense woods nearby. His short stocky figure was capable of small bursts of speed, but his legs were more used to the deck of a ship than tearing through the thorny shrubs and tangled tree roots of the forest floor. Timing his move, he vaulted the wall and sprinted across the open ground and into the waiting cover of the trees. He sank down behind a hawthorn bush that provided some concealment while he caught his heaving breath and listened intently. There was almost no sound at all. Strange, this area should be teaming with quail and other animals. Why were there so many men in the forest? Ah, they must be beaters for a hunting party nearby. The beaters were likely in search of the fat speckled quail that would be hiding among the dense undergrowth and in the surrounding fields.

James was hunting for a very different form of prey. He checked the five-shot Webley revolver in his coat, making sure it was fully loaded. It was an inexpensive sidearm, but it had served him well over the years. The last time he faced his quarry it escaped unscathed. That was a mistake he would correct today—or die trying.

The men moved off towards the fields, so James quietly advanced to the edge of the trees to get a closer look at the light-brown country house. The architecture was in the Palladian style, with symmetrical pillars in the front and circular arches over the large windows. There were multiple wings attached to the central house, and they too were adorned with pediments and porticos.

He was about ten meters away but, with the low fog on the ground, it was difficult to see clearly. As he stood behind a thick oak tree, he leaned outward and peered into the windows of the building. The first and second rooms proved empty and he quickly moved on. The third contained a large gathering, with all sorts of people moving about inside, but his target could not be seen there. At the last window on the side of the house, he was shocked to see the very face he had been searching for looking directly back at him. He leaped backward and turned sideways to conceal his broad shoulders behind the tree. He desperately hoped that he hadn't been seen. Maybe the eyes were simply looking out at the surrounding woods. No, that was foolish—he had been spotted. But, perhaps he could draw his prey to him instead. Risking another glance around the tree, he saw that the face had disappeared from the window. If he was discovered, he would do whatever was required to find a way to spring his trap, even if it cost him everything. Failing that, he would wait for another opportunity to take his revenge.

He had been away at a distant port when the letter came bearing news that would change his life forever. From that moment, James had vowed vengeance and thought of little else. He had been hunting for years now with only one previous encounter with his prey. That time he had lost his nerve. But now he would finally finish it. A little patience would cost him nothing and would be well worth the wait to end that particular life.

After several minutes with no alarm being sounded, he gradually retreated and moved deeper into the forest to wait. Nearly a quarter-hour of time passed. He snapped his head up abruptly as a faint scraping sound announced the approach of someone nearby. James cocked the hammer of his revolver and pointed it in the direction he had taken back from the house. Minutes passed in deafening silence as his heart thudded rapidly in his chest. There was no one there.

The attack came from his side instead of the front. James was completely unprepared by the sheer force of whatever hit him and knocked him sideways onto the ground. He only had a sense of a large dark shape as it continued the attack, falling upon him. Desperately, James brought his revolver to bear and fired a shot in the center of the enormous shape. A sound of pure fury exploded from the thing as a massive, clawed hand raked a fire of agony and blood across his outstretched arm and sent his revolver smashing through the dense brush. James tried to rise to his feet, but more burning pain blossomed in his chest and stomach. The terrible strength of the creature forced him down, crushing the breath from his lungs. He saw sharp canines and the hairy muzzle of a wolf as it slammed into his face and neck. He could only scream in surprise and disbelief as the foul-smelling animal ripped into his body and life began leaking out from him. His last fading thoughts were of his terrible failure and the unjustness of the world. This impossible creature had inexplicably killed him and prevented him from taking his revenge. He would never have the satisfaction of ending the life of the man whose face he had seen staring back at him through the country house window.

CHAPTER 1.

THE WOLF PUP

Despite the general calm of the country air and the purposeful seclusion of her art studio, Sage Holdsworth was having a difficult time focusing on her latest composition. It wasn't caused by the faint tangy fragrance of the Hookah smoke which wafted slowly upwards to the high wooden beams. Nor was the distraction coming from the plush, inviting pillows of the Chesterfield sofa where Lady Helena was lying seductively—as she was wont to do. Nor was it the dull throb of Sage's lingering migraine. Amazingly, it wasn't even the subject of the work itself that was causing the issue. No, the subject was more than fine, perfect and beautiful and distracting in its own way. The problem preventing her from continuing her painting was the soft and persistent whining coming from behind the heavy-oak door to the kitchen.

Sage put down her mahogany palette and sable brushes. They were extensions of her own hands and encrusted from heavy use, but still the finest that money could buy. Looking over at Lady Helena's relaxed form, she was struck with a moment of envy at her generous curves and glowing skin that was delicate and firm despite a life that would invite an onslaught of wrinkles to a normal woman. The woman's right hand seemed to point to her revealing bust line, while her left hand was thrown casually above her beautiful and regal face. Her heavy-lidded lashes revealed fiery and mischievous eyes which were set above full pink lips that were currently pursed in a slight smirk.

Sage shook off the feeling of inadequacy that came from comparing her own mousy brown hair and plain face to that of her friend. She shot her an imploring look. "Helena, please. Do something about the pup's crying. I'm trying to concentrate."

"Why should it be my job? It's your silly sense of charity that took that ridiculous pup in." Lady Helena sat up slowly and casually tossed back her long, obsidian-silk hair. "You must know that someday, that wolf cub will grow up into the beast that its mother was."

Sage tried to ignore the flash of blood, as the image of the giant grey wolf rushed back into her mind. During one of her nightly gatherings in Epping Forest, she was astounded to come across the animal—which was thought to have been hunted to extinction in England well over two centuries ago. She was at a loss to explain what her eyes saw. Perhaps it had escaped from a zoo.

Sage timidly approached the wolf mother, already dead

from starvation and caught in the metal leg hold fox trap that had cruelly ended the animal's life. Somehow, the grey wolf pup had been spared and the tiny creature sat crying next to the motionless form of his mother. The small animal also had a large gash on its paw, as if cut while trying to free the mother from the trap. Perhaps the mother had continued to suckle the wolf pup, even as she starved. It was a tragic loss, as the majestic animals no longer roamed the mighty forests and were even quite rare to see in captivity. Luckily, that evening she hadn't been alone but had taken along Dorian Gray for the first time.

Upon seeing the animals, wonderful kind-hearted Dorian had forgotten all about his trepidation of tramping through the damp forest at night. He had reluctantly agreed to help search for herbs that Sage needed for her paints. She would only allow paints that she mixed herself to touch her prized brushes and expensive canvases. The herbs were necessary to bring out the brilliant colors that distinguished her lifelike and compelling style. They gave the images a certain power—and they had other uses as well.

Her knowledge of herbs was of no help to the wolf mother. She was already gone as Dorian set his powerful arms to unhinging the fox trap. The hinge of the trap cracked and it broke, scoring a nasty gash across his hand—which he nobly ignored. Dorian gently lifted the lifeless form of the mother free and insisted on digging a hole in order to bury the she-wolf beneath the soft forest floor himself. He had been concerned for the small wolf pup and hugged it to his chest as the two walked through the trees and back to her studio. He patiently allowed the tiny animal to lick the blood that was freely flowing from the gash on his hand. At the sight of it he simply laughed merrily, amused at the apparent hunger the pup showed in response to the warm blood. Sage had almost warned him then, but instead seized on the adoring look in his endless blue eyes and offered to raise the pup herself. Turning it over to a zoo or conservatory seemed cruel. The animal could very well be the last of its kind and Sage hoped to one day release it back into the forest when it reached adulthood. She tenderly treated the uneven wounds that the jagged teeth of the fox trap had caused to the small grey paw. Sage dressed the injury with some dry bandages, staunching the surprisingly large flow of deep, red blood and treated it with an extract of coal tar. She would ensure that the wound healed properly and nurse the animal back to full health. That way, Dorian could visit as often as he liked and the two of them could play with the little whelp together for hours on end—and that suited her just fine.

With a sigh, Sage dragged herself away from the easel and walked towards the kitchen. As the bulky door swung open, the wolf pup ran out and went tumbling in a ball of fluff. It was still unsure of itself in this new environment and adorably sniffed around before retreating to the protection her legs offered. Unable to help herself, Sage giggled and scooped him up, planting a kiss on the soft, furry head. In that moment her migraine cleared and she hugged the animal and whispered to him. "Being adorable is another thing you share with him. That and also being grey. So, that is what I will call you, little Dorian Grey."

After finding a few bloody scraps of rabbit meat in the ice box, which the small wolf eagerly scarfed down, she changed the bandages on the injured paw. There was still a small amount of blood, slowly seeping out from the deep cuts on the tiny paw. She dabbed these and then re-bandaged the wound gingerly. Then she picked the small animal back up and exited the kitchen, depositing him in a shabby old dog bed by the roaring red fireplace. This way he would be within eyesight but safely away from her antique easel. Hopefully the fresh meat and warmth from the hearth would soon sooth the trying animal to sleep and prevent him from getting into any more trouble.

As she returned to her paint-smattered palette and darkened brushes, she placed the bloody bandages near her materials. Her aesthetic gaze took in how much more vibrant the crisp colors were on the changed bandage. She fancied how much closer she could get the current mixture on her palette to the color of Dorian's lips, if she only mixed in a few drops of the red blood. On a whim, she swirled her brush in the bloody bandage, and mixed it with the colors on her palette, before using the brush to apply it to the canvas. She stubbornly ignored the nagging sensation at the back of her mind that attempted to disrupt her creativity with annoying warnings. As she finished applying the new paint mixture, she noticed Lady Helena was no longer spread out in her feline pose, but was now admiring the canvas with a seriousness and focus that she had rarely observed from the socialite.

Lady Helena leaned forward to inspect the canvas. "This is your finest work, Sage. Easily the best that I have ever seen. You really must exhibit this at Colnaghi's gallery! Or, we can open a new one together, like I've been begging you to do for years now. Just imagine, our own darling gallery set along Dover Street or by the Berkeley Square gardens. I'll front the money if that's what it takes. Art like this must be seen and appreciated!"

Since they first met, Lady Helena had been trying to convince Sage that the two should open up an art gallery and go into business together. Sage appreciated her friendship and that Lady Helena had taken her under her wing, but she couldn't help but feel it was at least partly done because it was considered fashionable to be friends with a well-known artist. She often felt paraded around like a trained monkey at the various social events organized by Lady Helena, but was too shy to risk losing her friendship by complaining about it. She didn't mind having her work publicly praised by her friend, even if Lady Helena managed to somehow take credit for most of it. She always had been an overbearing person, as her husband knew well. Lady Helena all but ran her husband's flourishing trading company. She was the true mind behind the intricate business deals, the complicated purchase decisions, establishing trade routes, and managing contacts. Her husband was remanded to a figurehead, who merely signed the contracts that were put in front of him and provided any financial backing that was needed. This arrangement allowed Lady Helena to be very free with her spending, including her famously generous support for the arts.

Sage scowled. "Not this one." She formed her face into the familiar stubborn look which Lady Helena knew meant she might as well give up the argument now—for Sage would never change her mind.

"Are you sure? My dear, have you lost your mind entirely? This would elevate your fame to a level of international renown. I don't understand you artist types; so quick to create a masterpiece, then you go and hide it away under a mattress. If you won't display it, at least let me purchase it from you. Name your price, I'll pay a considerable sum for it."

"I can't, this painting is not for sale or for display."

Lady Helena sat down on the sofa and crossed her long, smooth legs slowly, fixing Sage with a momentary brooding glare. It lasted only for a few seconds before she was laughing in glittering tones. "Why ever not?"

"You'll tease me, but it's just too important to me. I've put too much of who I am into it."

Lady Helena scoffed. "Too much of who you are? My, you are vain—besides you aren't even in the painting. It's just that admittedly striking wolf pup and the most chiseled, intriguingly handsome young Greek god that I have ever beheld. Why, I do believe with those steely blue eyes and those golden locks, no man can be more beguiling."

"Yes," Sage admitted, "Mr. Gray is the most astounding man and quite difficult to look away from."

"Mr. Gray? Wait, you mean there is an actual living person who looks this good and I haven't met him? Where have you been hiding him, you naughty girl?"

Sage rolled her eyes. "I haven't been hiding him. I was just enjoying spending time with a new friend and didn't want him exposed to the terrible social scene that we have here so soon."

Lady Helena placed a bejeweled hand innocently over her ample chest. "My dear, I am a happily married woman you know, he has nothing to fear from the likes of me! Although, fear can be an important sign that you are doing the right thing. It is far more fun to do something, than to be constantly afraid of it. To not do something because of fear is really just a deception of self."

She paused to examine the expensive ring on her finger. "That is the beauty in being married, the necessity for deception by both spouses. Why, my Lord Husband has no clue what I am doing right now or where I will be later this evening, and it takes at least a few probing questions for me to discover his whereabouts—were I so inclined. But we do so often see each other at a Gala or fundraiser and the occasional dinner, of course. Now I am rambling, tell me about this astonishing young man that you have been keeping all for yourself."

Sage sat down next to Lady Helena, excited to relate the tale of her first encounter with the intriguing man in the painting and unable to resist her conspirators tone.

"It was three months ago at a crowded gallery opening across town. I was having some of my minor works from my Realism period exhibited and was required to make an appearance. I was bored to tears after ten minutes of trying to follow the tedious conversation and limp Hors d'oeuvres. Then I felt someone's eyes on me from across the room. You know that itchy, ghosts-on-your-neck feeling? I looked to the side and saw him standing there, just looking at me. Oh how I must have made a fool of myself. When our eyes met I stopped breathing and I was terrified. I felt like my whole soul was drained and taken in at that one look from him. His face was art itself, with a jaw hewn from mythology. His figure was a bronze statue of perfection, and an aura of charisma glowed off of him. It felt like my life was fated to that one moment, that one meeting."

Sage began picking nervously at the stich work of the

sofa. "I was petrified and tried to turn to leave. Then he started walking towards me, with that boyish grin on his face and my feet became frozen in place, as if by an icy glacier. He approached confidently, introduced himself with a courtly bow, and said that he had been waiting all evening just to meet me. Me of all people! He went on to say that my art had inspired him. We talked for hours about art and the various compositions that were on display. He always had a warm smile on his lips and laughed so easily. We had an immediate connection and were friends at once. That was the first time I met Dorian Gray."

Lady Helena cocked her head to the side in a distinctively bird-like expression and gave her a calculating look. "Tell me more about this Mr. Gray. How often do you see him?"

"Nearly every day! It makes me so happy to see him and he sits for my painting for hours."

"Why Sage, I thought only your art brought you happiness?"

"He is like art, and our time together fills me with more inspiration than I have ever felt before. All of my work is suddenly electrifying!"

"Tell me, is he very fond of you?"

Sage considered this question for a few moments. "He likes me. I know he likes me. I do compliment him too much and find myself telling him things I have never told anyone—

which he must find tedious. We sit and talk of everything and he is very charming towards me, although he does tend to say thoughtless and hurtful things quite carelessly. But I am sure he doesn't mean any of them. I feel like I've opened my whole self to him, but I am nothing more than a curiosity or artistic indulgence in return, like a decoration which suits his vanity."

"Don't worry my dear, an artistic genius with your talents will soon find inspiration elsewhere. I am sure you will expeditiously tire of the whole thing long before he does. Men are fickle creatures and are too easily distracted by the next shiny bauble, or whatever curvaceous set of hips walks in front of them next. You mustn't let him think you are too interested, or he will mistreat you. Try ignoring him a little, or being cold to him the next time you meet. That always does wonders for romance. If you go in for that sort of thing. Maybe I can help."

"I don't want you to meet him."

"Why ever not?"

"Dorian is my dearest friend. He is kind and has a pure soul and a simple nature. You'll try to influence him or spoil him somehow. This is the one person who adds more to my art then I could ever explain and I couldn't stand to lose him."

Suddenly there was a ring at the door, followed by the elderly butler entering and announcing, "Mr. Dorian Gray has arrived to see you, my lady."

CHAPTER 2.

DORIAN GRAY

As Sage put her hand to the door of the parlor she turned back to Lady Helena. "I am trusting you." She fixed her with a glare then slowly opened the door. "Dorian, hello! You are just in time to sit for me a bit longer as I finish".

"I am so tired of sitting. Let's do something fun today instead, oh," he trailed off as his gaze took in Lady Helena's alluring figure standing in the background. "I didn't realize you weren't alone." A slight bit of color reached his cheeks as his eyes traveled her enticing torso.

"Dorian, I would like to introduce my good friend Lady Helena Wotton to you. Lady Helena, this is Mr. Gray."

Lady Helena slowly strode forward, with a distinctive sway to her hips as she bowed her head gracefully. "A pleasure to meet you, Mr. Gray. Sweet Sage here has been telling me about how the two of you met, but I am afraid I have so little other useful information. Pray tell me, what do you do for a living?"

Dorian paused with a sudden frown reaching his face. After a brief second it disappeared and he gave a handsome bow. "A pleasure to make your acquaintance, Lady Wotton. As to my profession, well, I am a musician you see, but really I dabble in quite a few things including philanthropy for theatre and the arts mainly—oh yes, and also the operation of my late father's business."

A certain naive look that was yearning for approval reached the bold-blue eyes, as the shiny, blond-haired head remained slightly inclined.

Lady Helena took it all in at once and immediately understood the youth and the purity, the face that inspired trust and trusted immediately, the impeccably sharp and expensive clothing, the demeanor of a young man who had been raised by his mother alone—until she too had passed away, leaving him flush with cash from a trust fund that had been endowed by his deceased father's business. No wonder Sage worshipped him.

"You are far too charming for philanthropy, Mr. Gray. Please do call me Lady Helena, I insist." Helena cooed as she took a long cigarette from her purse and placed it suggestively between her lips before igniting it. "Lady Wotton was my overbearing mother-in-law, may she rest in peace."

"Dorian," Sage interrupted, "come sit for me so I can finish your painting today. Helena, it was nice seeing you but we really must finish. I hope you don't mind leaving so soon, I don't mean to be rude." She immediately moved out of the parlor and to her art studio. She stopped by her easel and began mixing paints and preparing her brushes.

Dorian and Lady Helena both followed her into the room. "Oh, no Lady Helena, please don't leave—we have only just met. I think Sage is just in one of her bad moods, and it would be nice to have someone to talk with while she paints. She concentrates so much that she absolutely refuses to speak a word and it gets quite dull. Besides, I am intrigued to hear why you think I am not well suited for philanthropy. You don't mind do you Sage? It would be nice for me to have someone to talk to while you work."

Lady Helena sat back down on the sofa, flicking ash recklessly towards a bowl—*that was definitely NOT an ashtray*, while managing to show even more cleavage.

"I suppose it would be alright if it helps Dorian sit still. Then you must stay, of course."

"Well, I would but I am afraid I have some pressing business of my own and must be leaving. I am meeting an associate at the Orleans."

Dorian's eyes widened at that and his jaw tightened with resolution. "Sage, if Lady Helena must leave, then so too will I, for it does get dreadfully boring. You must ask her to stay."

Sage surrendered to his stately petition immediately.

"Very well then, please stay—I insist. Surely you could reschedule and meet this associate of yours at another time?"

Lady Helena gave a reproachful look. "Very well, if I must. I suppose I can send him a letter through my valet, begging his forgiveness and propose that we meet later this evening."

"Perfect!" Dorian's face lit up with a broad smile and he strode confidently towards the fireplace while removing his tailored jacket. "And how is my sleepy little wolf doing today? Have you eaten well? Wake up sleepy one, it is time for us to sit for Sage while she paints. Then, maybe you can have some treats!"

Dorian lifted the wolf out of the chewed dog bed, to excited yips and licks all over his face and hands. He laughed playfully as he seated himself, and the two turned towards the easel, assuming a comfortable position. "Lady Helena, have you met my wolf pup? *He* thinks I am well suited for philanthropy. Don't you boy?"

Lady Helena laughed in an inviting manner. "Why my dear, you do have a clever wit about you. I will tell you my thoughts on philanthropy. You see, there is far too much danger of influencing people in philanthropy. To influence someone, is to give them a piece of your soul. Then that person's passions and thoughts are no longer their own. Their sins—if there is such a thing as sin, are but a borrowed thing. Their music, is but a recording of the real notes and they are but actors, playing a role for which they themselves were not written."

Lady Helena paused to make sure she still had everyone's attention and smoothed her dress, before reclining further and continuing on in a thoughtful tone. "The purpose of life is to develop and grow, to reach the heights of one's potential, and to experience all the pleasures and joys that this existence has to offer. To do that, you must understand your own nature. This can be a difficult process involving extensive experimentation and exploration—sometimes even pain. People are too afraid to learn about their true selves and thus they never understand the meaning and value of their lives. Courage in the face of fear has fled society and people are governed only by an outdated sense of moral and religious ideals."

Sage spoke without taking her eyes from the canvas. "Dorian, turn your head a little to the side and try to hold that fuzzy trickster still. No, to the other side. Perfect."

"And so," Lady Helena went on in a musical voice, ignoring the interruption, "I believe if a man were brave enough, he would live his life to the fullest and most complete level—then he would experience every feeling and thought, every dream and beauty, and every impulse and joy possible. At that point he would no longer fear himself, but truly understand his own mind and the essence of his body. There would be no purity or sin, only the memory of pleasure or the luxury of regret. For temptations are only ended when you give into them."

Lady Helena let that thought sink in, while looking on with half-lidded eyes and slowly stroking her fingertips along her leg and thigh. She delivered Dorian a seductive look that would quicken any man's pulse. "The sickness of longing can be cleansed from the soul only by not forbidding anything from yourself—despite invasive laws or societal norms. And of course, this all begins in the mind. Surely, Mr. Gray, you have had unfulfilled passions or thoughts that have made you afraid to act or limited your experiences. Tell me, do they come to you through brief day dreams or by means of extended nighttime fantasies?"

Dorian's face once again colored, as he struggled to respond in a coherent sentence. "I, well, I have never heard things explained in that way before or thought about them in such a manner." Dorian glanced out of the open window and out at the trees with a thoughtful look.

Lady Helena could tell that he was considering her words carefully. His hands moved in an absent-minded way in response to the furious, tiny wolf as it tumbled and chewed on anything within reach. A full two minutes passed in near-silence, save for the scrape of Sage's painting knife and the sandpapery-slide of her brush strokes.

Lady Helena spoke up again in silvery tones that made her flirtation clear. "You really do have a wonderful and classic profile Mr. Gray. I hope you endeavor to shade yourself from the sun."

Dorian gave a cheeky smile. "What does it matter, a little sun can't hurt."

"It should matter to you. Your youth is a treasure, the one treasure worth having."

"Isn't there so much more to life than youth, Lady Helena?"

"Ah, NOW you are inundated with an endless stream of senses to feed the soul. But one day, you will be old and wrinkled and ugly, with your forehead creased with lines, your lips cracked and scarred, and you will feel the weight of age in your very bones. Then you will understand my point. For now, a face such as yours could change the world, but will it always be that way?"

Lady Helena stood and boldly extended her hand, stopping just short of caressing his cheek. "Remember Mr. Gray, a flower dies when first it begins to bud. There are only a few years left for you to truly live fully and in the moment. Every day, your youth fades a little more and you come closer to death's door. So, cherish your youth while you have it and do not squander a single moment. Even love is merely a mixture of pheromones and physiology. Most young men can't help themselves, nor control their actions when it comes to a willing and suited partner. Why limit yourself to experiencing love only once—or only a few times? Live your life and seek out new sensations while fearing nothing! For there is nothing you could not do. The world is your oyster for but a few seasons more. Do not waste that time, for you can never have it back."

As she spoke, Dorian's eyes grew larger—not only with a little fear, but also with a certain determination.

Sage noisily put down her palette and brush. "There! I have finally finished!"

Lady Helena rushed over to examine the picture. She gave an appreciative murmur and her eyes seemed glued to the finished work. It was an amazing likeness and an astounding work of art. Lady Helena touched her hand to her heart and spoke in a hushed tone. "Sage, well done. This is the finest portrait I have ever seen. Mr. Gray, come take a look for yourself."

As Dorian gazed upon his own visage his lips slowly curled upward in a smile of pleasure. A look of admiration and joy came to his eyes as he stared raptly at the image before him, completely motionless. Something stirred deep inside for the first time. A comprehension of the real artistic qualities of his own face as others must see it. He saw his face now with all its beauty and attractiveness but, in his mind's eye, he also saw an image of how that same face would one day look. He imagined the skin wrinkled and grey, the eyes dimmer and faded of color, the strong figure bent and broken, and the life of his soul—gone from that body. He would one day be hideous and disgusting. Pain like a knife struck his heart and he felt a hand of ice squeeze his lungs like a vise.

Dorian closed his eyes and whispered in a low voice. "How sad that one day I will grow old, but the man in this picture will always remain young. He will never age even a single day. Even this young pup has years to grow into a majestic wolf, but I will soon grow old and look horrible as time ravages me. It isn't fair that we have only a few short years. If only I could remain young forever, I would give anything!"

Sage approached him and reached out for his hand. "Dorian, it isn't as bad as all that."

But Dorian drew his hand away. "No! If I could be young eternally, I would give my very soul!" He turned away, his cheeks burning and face hot.

Sage fixed Lady Helena with an angry look and crossed her arms. "This is your doing."

Lady Helena merely shrugged and went back to her cigarette. "This is just the real Dorian Gray. But enough of this painting, let us all go to the theatre tonight!"

At that suggestion Dorian seemed to regain his composure. He loved the artistry and music of the theatre above all else. His mood lightened and he relaxed his shoulders from their rigid position. "That is a wonderful idea. I would love to go to the theatre with you Lady Helena. Sage you should come with us."

"I can't really. I have too much work to do here. Why

don't you stay here with me instead? Or if you must go, then promise me you will come visit tomorrow."

Dorian nodded his head. "You have my word Sage."

Lady Helena smiled at him meaningfully. "Well then Mr. Gray, it seems I must reschedule with my business associate. You and I shall have to go it alone."

CHAPTER 3.

AN AWAKENING

Dorian had visited many theatres before and been invited to many private boxes, but never one quite as grand and luxurious as the one Lady Helena now led him to. It was situated in the finest area of London, where the wealthy and powerful conjugated and reveled in extravagance. The playhouse itself was one of the newer constructions and was built to accommodate very large audiences. The front displayed several ornate facades and four tall stone columns with a large glazed dome set in the center of the building. The inside of the three-story building was brightened by the most decorative gas lighting and the eyes feasted on all the bright fabrics and intriguing paintings that adorned the walls. Under the dome were three elaborate balcony areas surrounding an enlarged pit which was sunken below street level.

The house was packed that night with the most influential and beautiful denizens that the city had to offer. They were greeted at an exclusive wide-oaken door and quickly passed through to the private level via the lavish grand staircase where they were met with sumptuous, thick carpets imported from all over the world, gold-tooled leather, and plush furniture.

Despite the heavy cloud of smoke that hung in the air, Dorian was easily able to distinguish several seating areas where the acquaintances and business associates of Lady Helena gathered. During intermissions, the group purposefully ignored the detailed scene the backdrops painted upon the stage, preferring to attend to their own various indulgences. Only when the actors took the stage did they give their attentions to the portrayal of Shakespeare's "A Midsummer Night's Dream." It seemed to Dorian, that the scenes both on the stage and between the acts in the private box played out in parallel; with multiple ladies wearing dresses of every shape and color, gentlemen both tall and fat, high-priced prostitutes, and shrewd businessmen mingling and trading affection. This was all done while smoking tangy cigars and poignant cigarettes, drinking dark-swirling liquors, and engaging in several other types of discourteous displays. When the play resumed and the audience took their seats, the actors playing Lysander, Hermia, Helena, and Demetrius capered and courted, fought and fled. And of course, true to both scenes—all loved Helena and Lady Helena alike.

Lady Helena graciously received and dismissed her enamored guests each in turn, keeping Mr. Gray at her side and making the necessary introductions. Many were business associates that sought her expertise and skill at importing or exporting various desirable items, but more still were admirers or social acquaintances looking to bask in the limelight and earn a place at the heart of the action. All were immediately enamored with him and fell over themselves to obtain his approval.

This was all quite new for Mr. Gray, but he played his part well, with a warm smile and welcoming voice. Ladies and harlots alike sought his favor and attentions as surely as Puck sought mischief in the dark forests that were his domain. Lady Helena presided over it all like royalty, as if entertaining international dignitaries at her summer court. She controlled the situation carefully, allowing Mr. Gray a brief smoke of a fine, imported cigar from Lady Weller here, a drink of single malt Scotch from Mr. Harrop there, and a few moments with a dollymop sitting on his lap—quickly shoed away after an unexpected, lingering kiss. The people and music became a blur of mixed sensations, intriguing sights, and unfamiliar sounds.

As Dorian reached for a proffered glass of fine Cognac, Lady Helena scolded him gently and laid her hand on top of his. "Have a care Mr. Gray, it would be in poor taste to dull your senses too soon to the pleasures this night holds for you. One must build their tolerance for liquor slowly and gain mastery of it for what it is: A tool to ease your mind and nerves yes, but when correctly applied—a powerful means of persuasion in both business and romance."

Dorian nodded and found wisdom in Lady Helena's words, as he did to every new idea she exposed his receptive mind to.

When the play concluded and the actors made their final bows, Lady Helena whisked the select few downstairs to a fleet of waiting carriages. These carried them covertly to the private and infamous club owned by Mr. Harrop. There Dorian was both shocked and intrigued to observe a provocative production of Victorian Burlesque, as it progressed through the night.

The performers were beautiful and sultry and graceful nonetheless. Misted with the most intriguing scent and adorned in deep, scarlet-red corsets, with dark opaque stockings, they were covered in sparkling stones as well as fanciful plumes of feathers which they employed to cover—or not cover, various areas of their athletic bodies as they cavorted, danced, and sang in beautiful voices.

Like a siren's call, he was drawn to them by the harmonious melodies of their song and the undulating rhythm of their bodies, as abstruse music and swaying dance intertwined in a carnival for the senses. Dorian and Lady Helena were seated at a place of honor to enjoy the spectacle. They were plied with a steady stream of mysterious drinks and enticing female companionship, who became evermore bold and free with their hands and attentions as the evening waned on. Dorian quickly squashed any moral objections nagging restlessly at the back of his mind as he observed the other businessmen, gentlemen, and even ladies of high society engaging in the debauchery with high abandon.

The men had been joined in secret by many of the ladies from the theatre. The majority seemed to be in attendance without their husbands and arrived by separate carriages. Neither seemed to have any qualms about enjoying themselves, nor the dancer's advances.

The dancers would approach first Lady Helena, then Dorian, one at a time. They flirted, shared a drink, and often reclined across a chair or sofa while conversing. Several seated themselves on Dorian's lap directly and one even conducted a private display of her dancing prowess while still seated there. This kept Dorian's interest most keenly, though Lady Helena soon became bored and began a lengthy conversation with Mr. Harrop which crossed to and fro between business, art and music.

It was most difficult to sort out the time from the jeweled pocket watch that Dorian kept under his waist coat. It ticked sluggishly and stuttered back and forth between two hands and four. Uncertain on his feet and reeling at the overstimulation of his senses, Dorian thought it best to beg a hasty retreat.

He struggled with the amount of drink weighing on his

mind. His thoughts seemed liquefied and he felt as though he were aboard a mighty ship, the room swaying from side to side with the waves of intoxication. "Lady Helena, the time being half past three, I really must retire for the evening. I thank you so much for your gracious invitation and...entertainments."

"The pleasure was mine, Mr. Gray. It was about time you were properly introduced to society. I look forward to the next evening we shall share together. Allow me to take you home as it seems you have had a bit too much to drink."

"No, no that is quite alright."

"Well at least let my valet escort you in the carriage, it is my duty as your hostess to see that you make it safely home."

"Very well, perhaps that would be wise."

Dorian made his farewells and struggled towards the carriage with the help of Lady Helena's valet. Her man helped him into the carriage and quickly started the horses moving at a brisk walk. It seemed only moments until Dorian arrived back at his father's house.

It had been many years since his father passed away, yet still he was unable to think of the large country house in Woodford as his own property. A great deal of expense had gone towards the rejuvenation of the garden and the revitalization of the exterior of the building, as well to refurnish and style of the interior to Dorian's tastes.

He refused further help from the valet, making his own way up the walkway towards his father's manor, partly so he would be unobserved as he retched in the concealing dark of the garden flowerbeds. Afterward, his mind felt greatly cleared—yet still troubled as the evening's events replayed themselves through his memory. His dutiful valet, Henry, was not unaccustomed to late hours and had everything prepared so Dorian could be quickly abed. His last thoughts as sleep overtook him were of Lady Helena's dangerous smile and how displeased Sage would be if she ever learned of his questionable behavior that evening.

Late the next day, Dorian was awoken by the most astounding headache and overwhelming feelings of guilt. Despite the onslaught against his psyche, he arose and began dressing with some difficulty. His eyes were sensitive to the light from the windows and his stomach churned with emptiness. He began a prolonged breakfast of delicate biscuits and butter along with a heaping of bacon and strong coffee thoughtfully brought by Henry.

After the meal he felt much improved and he slowly made his way to visit Sage and the wolf pup as promised. Sage was most pleased to see him as always and was easily steered away from any conversation about last night's misadventures. The pup seemed greatly grown in both size and confidence as it bounded around the entire house, exploring new areas and greeting all imagined combatants, such as the Victorian reading chair, with a vigorous energy. It was good to see the two and the whole experience cleared his mind from the foggy and conflicting thoughts lurking there. The wolf pup was most loyal, barely leaving his side, and quite in tune with Dorian as they played and wrestled—for the two had forged a lasting bond.

As the days of summer quickly expired, this ritual would repeat itself frequently. Dorian continued experiencing new discoveries and delights of the night at the instructional hand of Lady Helena. Occasionally, he would accept her offers to escort him home. Those moments spent alone with his friend and mentor were most informative, with Dorian quickly mastering an understanding of the female mind and body. Lady Helena insisted that each time had been but a drunken mistake and would not be repeated again—until the next time. And in each instance, on the following morning, Dorian would rise and seek a sort of purification and atonement spent in innocence, simplicity, and playfulness with the wolf pup and Sage at her art studio. The two would converse for long hours on all manner of subjects—including Lady Helena's past.

CHAPTER 4.

LADY HELENA

Helena Rivera's mother had passed away just before her eighth birthday. She had loved her mother dearly, and the memories of their brief time spent together singing light-hearted songs and silly-dancing in the rain still caused her great pain. So much so, that she refused to be addressed as Lady Rivera. When someone did address her in that manner she would grow haughty, saying, "Lady Rivera was my mother. No other can possibly be worthy of that name, so I insist you call me Lady Helena."

Like her mother, Helena was gifted with long, thin legs and a delicate figure. Her dark, smoldering eyes and silky onyx hair drew a great deal of attention from the boys, which only increased with time—as did her bust line and her need for that attention. Her father, Lord Rivera, had little time for his daughter as he was a very successful businessman. He was often busy forming complicated deals and frequently away from home. Helena soon discovered that the best way to spend time with him was to take an interest in his work and travel with him on his business trips.

She showed a keen mind for figures, and a natural ability to read others. This proved vital in assisting her father in his many business dealings. Helena would smile shyly and flirt to distract his gentlemen associates, while her father maneuvered the deal to his favor. She observed everything carefully and redirected their attentions expertly. It was no surprise then, when Helena announced that she would be attending school with the goal of improving her business acumen. Her father gave his blessing, and promised to arrange for her to reside in luxurious apartments near the school of her choosing.

At the age of seventeen, she began her enrollment at North London Collegiate School for Women. The school had only just recently opened, and was the first of its kind to teach the higher learning of mathematics and Latin to females.

It only took about a semester for Helena to become bored with her classes and fall into the wrong crowd of friends, bent on obtaining the affections of a group of audacious and politically motivated gentlemen who called themselves the London Ricardian Artists Society.

Joel Guyet was the brazen leader of the group, having the distinction of previously living in France, and some minor training under his father—who was also a painter. Since he likewise had the most notorious reputation as a socialist and troublemaker, he and Helena quickly became fast friends. The two attended a number of political protests together, leaving Helena greatly impressed with Joel's ideas on social, political, and economic reform. It was only natural that Joel would suggest Helena pose for his paintings in the nude. This happened regularly, though few of the paintings were ever finished before Joel would throw aside his brushes and take Helena to his bed. She was still young and naïve and before she knew what was happening, she had fallen for the young artist. But Helena was about to learn her first lesson about love.

When not attending her classes, she spent her free time posing for his paintings, or the two discussed the upcoming forms of art and music. They regularly attended the theatre together and could often be found at some small art gallery. At night, the two stayed out late with friends, drinking wine and visiting various opium dens. Joel believed the opium opened his mind to the true meaning of life and the abstract beauty of the senses. Helena had tried the sickly-sweet smoke, but she couldn't abide how the haze made her mind flow slowly in any direction that it pleased. She preferred to have her wits sharp and be in control of the direction that her thoughts took. She favored the effects of cocaine, particularly when added to a cup of wine known as Vin Mariani wine.

One afternoon she returned home from school early when the day's classes were unexpectedly cancelled. She climbed the stairs to the spacious apartments that her father rented at considerable expense. Helena selected them because they overlooked a delightful little garden with a small, picturesque pond complete with tiny shimmering fish. From her window you could watch the white-cheeked Pintail ducks take flight as the golden sun rose over the water. The apartments themselves were warm and welcoming with rich, comfortable furniture and a small, convenient hearth. Joel had secretly moved in a few weeks ago while maintaining the façade of dwelling with his cousin. He claimed one of the bedrooms as his studio. The two shared the master bedroom and the small, but modern kitchen. Helena was as happy as she had ever been.

As she opened the door, she had an immediate feeling that something was wrong. Opium smoke hung heavy in the air. Joel knew he wasn't allowed to smoke in the apartment. She smiled as she imagined giving him a very stern talking to—then making up passionately after the inevitable fight. The door to Joel's studio was curiously closed. He usually liked to paint with all the doors and windows open to allow for as much light as possible. As Helena approached, she heard quiet sighs and a grunting that distinctly belonged to Joel. Flinging the door wide, she took in the scene. There was movement on the very sofa where she had posed for him and the two had made love together countless times. Joel looked up, mid-coitus with some young harlot, their clothes were strewn around the floor.

The strumpet quickly covered herself while Joel seemed confused and slow to move. "Helena! What are you doing home so early from class? I didn't think you'd be back this soon."

"Joel! How could you?"

"Calm down Helena, let's discuss this."

"Discuss? What is there to discuss?" With that, Helena strode across the room, opened the window, and began throwing Joel's clothing and paints outside.

The terrified girl on the sofa gathered what clothes she could and hastily retreated from the room. Joel could only offer up a wordless outrage as he struggled to dress.

"Run you tart!" Helena called after the fleeing girl, as she flung canvases and brushes out of the open window.

"Helena, it didn't mean anything," Joel began again in a detached tone.

"Well this should mean something. Get out! I never want to see you again you filthy bunter! Get out immediately, or ill cut off your tallywags and hang them from the roof."

Joel left, encouraged by the easel that Helena flung at his head. Now alone in the apartment, she broke down in tears and slid down to the floor, crying. Her breath caught as she looked up at the remaining canvas in the room. Wonderfully depicted in intricate detail, was the body of the naked whore who had just run from the room. Joel had actually finished the painting. That hurt more than anything else. In a rage, she rushed over and grabbed the canvas, intending to smash it over the desk—

but she couldn't bring herself to do it. It was beautifully done, likely Joel's best work. She could see the care and love in the brushstrokes. Sadly, she placed the canvas on the ground, where Joel could retrieve it. It would be a shame to destroy it.

For several more hours she wept, visiting each room of the apartments in turn—trying in vain to erase the memories the two had created there. The small kitchen where they had cooked breakfasts together, rainy nights spent wrapped in each other's arms in front of the fire, and passionate afternoons spent in amorous bliss.

She gathered her things, leaving the apartment and her schooling that same day to return to her father's home. As the years rolled by, she tried to dull the memories of the warm summer's days and cool winter evenings spent laughing and talking with Joel. A parade of other lovers almost did the trick. Helena kept her mind occupied, staying busy by helping her father with his business, and with various drugs and stimulants. Though bittersweet, she still loved art and the theatre and took in as much as she could.

When her father grew gravely ill one fall season, it became apparent that she would have to do something to prevent losing everything—including his business. Fortunately, the son of a long-standing trading partner of her father's named Lord Wotton had expressed interest in marriage. Before he died, her father blessed the match on the condition that his daughter be allowed to continue running the trading company that he had spent so many hard years building. Lord Wotton readily agreed, happy to attain such a beautiful bride. He might have reconsidered, had he been able to see the impenetrable walls that she had built around her fragile heart.

CHAPTER 5.

JULIET

In the early afternoon, nearly a month later, Dorian Gray reclined in a contemptuous leather armchair in Lady Helena's library as he sulked and waited for her return. The room was scattered with various works of art from Paris and Germany, oak paneling framing the ceiling, and heavy, imported Persian rugs adorning the floors. Flowers, bright in sapphire blue and crimson reds, sang out from every corner of the ornately decorated room. The only sounds came from the ancient grandfather clock as it chimed out the hours and from a gilded golden-wire cage in the corner where a curious red-plumed parrot jumped incessantly from perch to perch, between squawks of outrage.

Lady Helena was always late, likely coming from some meeting or lunch with her male business associates that she often disappeared with for hours at a time. Dorian was leafing through the numerous volumes of Greek tragedies, philosophical letters of Homer and Plato, and the various odd works Lady Helena was so fond of that challenged societies views of virtue and morality. At last, he heard echoing footsteps from the tiled hallway outside.

"Lady Helena, how discourteous you are to keep me waiting so long!"

But it was Lord Wotton who answered in a somewhat timid but smooth voice. "I am afraid it is not Lady Helena, Mr. Gray."

"I beg your pardon Lord Wotton, but it is a pleasure to see you as well."

"Ah, but it is I who must apologize Mr. Gray, for I have often seen you at the opera with my Lady wife and have been remiss in my attentions to you."

"Not at all Lord Wotton, I understand you are often busy with important matters of state and with your import and export business as well. I should have noticed you and took the initiative myself. It is only that I do so concentrate on the music, for one must never speak during good music, but truly listen to it with all of their senses attuned."

"That is one of Helena's views, is it not? I do hear so many of her views from her friends. It is the only way I come to know them. In truth my wife handles the affairs of the import and export business. She has quite the keen mind for it. You really must join me at one of my parties for entertaining foreign dignitaries sometime Mr. Gray. They can be a bit tedious sometimes with all of the politicians I must discourse with, but I assure you, I spare no expense for the entertainment—Ah! Here is my Lady wife now. Helena I have been meaning to ask you something—now I forget what it was."

Lady Helena greeted her husband with a kiss on the cheek. "My love, I am sure you will remember if you think on it, and we can discuss it at dinner later this evening. I am so sorry that I am late Mr. Gray."

"Well Mr. Gray, it has been a pleasure. I hope to see you at dinner later this evening. Goodbye Helena, I am sure I will remember what it was I wished to discuss with you by this evening." Lord Wotton hurried out of the room, lighting a fat cigar on his way.

"Never marry someone so sentimental. In fact, never marry at all. Men only ever marry because they are tired and disappointed, women only ever marry because they are curious what it would be like—and are also disappointed in what life has given them."

"I am not sure if I will marry, but if it is how you say, then I am too much in love to ever get married!"

Lady Helena lifted her hand to her face in surprise. "What's that? Who are you in love with?"

A crimson blush spread slowly across Dorian's face. "With an actress. She is the most amazing Juliet you have ever seen! Her name is Sibyl Vane and she is an undiscovered genius in a meager theatre near Walthamstow. I was strolling by it quite by accident after a recent foray in London. I had gotten quite lost and stumbled across the owner standing outside smoking a most vile cigar. As he saw me his eyes lit up, 'Have a box, m'Lord?' he said. And he would not take no for an answer, but whisked me inside the horrid little theatre. To think, I almost refused him. Had I not gone inside that day, I would have missed the most beautiful creature enact the greatest romance of my life."

Lady Helena forced a laugh between her delicate lips. "Mr. Gray, you should say the FIRST romance of your life, not the greatest, for you shall always be loved and be in love. This is merely the beginning of your foray into the complicated world of infatuation."

"I am not as shallow as all that. Now let me finish my tale. I tell you, my Juliet was a shining beacon in an otherwise third-rate and tawdry affair. The dingy gallery was full in contrast to the empty stalls, with a terrible smell about the air, and there was a most dreadful orchestra complete with cracked and rusty instruments. I was beginning to question what I was doing in that wretched hole, Romeo and Mercutio being played in a very poor style, but then Juliet emerged."

He paused and a beaming smile lit up Dorian's face as he remembered first seeing her.

"She appeared to be near seventeen years of age, but looked like a vision from the Greek tragedies. With plaited coils of dark luscious hair, lips like the petals of a rose, and large, deep eyes that contained all the delight of her passion. She was the loveliest girl I have ever seen in all my life. Then she spoke. I have never heard such a voice before. It seemed she was instantly Juliet. From deep tones to flute-like music like the lark, she spoke and sang her parts with an excitement that stirred the whole audience. She concluded to thunderous applause and I could barely contain my own appreciation."

Dorian paused again and closed his eyes. "When I close my eyes now, I can still hear her and picture her. The owner brought me back after the show to meet her. I remember I could hardly form a coherent sentence when first speaking to her. I was so enraptured by her beauty and presence."

"That doesn't sound like the Mr. Gray I know."

"Yes, I was quite flummoxed while we conversed. She asked me how I liked her rendition of Juliet and I could only stammer out my appreciation. Fortunately, she was very gracious and I was able to recover as we discussed the arts and various playwrights. I invited her to dine with me at the club but she refused, claiming that her mother expected her home promptly. I was quite bewildered and didn't know what to say next, until she said that she hoped I would come and see her again the next night. Of course, I agreed fervently."

Lady Helena was barely able to conceal her exaggerated eye-rolling as Dorian continued his tale.

"Every night since, for two weeks, I have been there to

see her performances. One night she is Rosalind, the next Imogen. What an actress she is Lady Helena! She is innocent and glamorous, mysterious and transfiguring. I love her with all my heart. I love her!"

"Well this Sibyl Vane sounds quite charming. Do tell me what your relations with the young girl are?"

A deep flush returned to Dorian's face and he was immediately outraged. "Lady Helena, that is quite private but I assure you she is sacred to me."

"Only the sacred things are worth touching. She will be yours one day."

"Oh, you are incorrigible. Perhaps it was the champagne, but I knew from the first night that I must get to know her more intimately. The owner wasted no time in regularly insisting I be brought backstage after the performance and introduced to all of the other actors. I do believe he hoped to recruit me as a benefactor for their troupe. Every time afterwards when we met, she was shy and gentle, and whenever I complemented her performance for the evening, her eyes would grow wide with wonder. She really has no notion of the power she holds over us all. Despite my assurances to the contrary, the owner kept referring to me as 'My Lord'. I assured Sibyl I was nothing of the sort. 'You look more like a prince. Prince Charming I will call you,' she said."

"Ah, she is smooth with her compliments."

"No, she was perfectly sincere. She is quite ignorant of

the world and really knows nothing of life. She lives with her faded old mother who once also was an actress in her younger days. Sibyl is quite divine though. I am forever longing to see her. That delightful talent hidden in that pretty, ivory body. You and Sage must come with me to see her. I shall find a way to take over her career and bring her out properly at the West End theatre. Then the whole world will come to love her as I do."

"Very well. Sage and I will join you at the eight o'clock show next week. But shouldn't you be the one to extend the invitation to dear Sage?"

"I have not laid eyes on her for a week. She even sent me the portrait she painted adorned in the most wonderfully designed frame. I feel quite horrid for ignoring her and the wolf so. He has grown much larger now and dominates the room with his wild and intelligent manner. Sage is really quite proud of how the animal has grown. Please extend my invitation to her tomorrow. I can't see her alone right now, she does say the most annoying things and gives me the most trying of advice."

"Sage puts all of her brilliance and charm into her work. As a consequence of her art, she has nothing of it left for her own life. For an artist must either be amazing in their work or in their pursuit of life, but it can never be both."

"I wonder if that is really so? It must be, if you say it. But I must be off. Do not forget about next week. Good-afternoon."

As Lady Helena was left alone with her thoughts, she

was not jealous in the least, but pleased by the progress Dorian had made in becoming more self-aware and open to all of the wonderful pleasures that the world had to offer. Even this silly infatuation with the young Sibyl was a vital part of his development. Men give the name of experience and wisdom to the mistakes that they inevitably make in life which are wholly necessary in forming their character. Yes, the lad was growing into quite the striking man and more fully coming into his own.

CHAPTER 6.

SIBYL VANE

The next night, as had become his custom, Dorian visited Sibyl at the theatre. He was seen as a regular and was well known by the staff. The coarse doorman greeted him with a nod and he was immediately escorted to his usual box by a bawdy steward that reeked of cheap wine. The steward promised to return shortly with the finest wine that the house had to offer—likely a third-rate vintage.

The private box was small and threadbare, with thinly padded cushions and a ratty rug on the floor that boasted a wide spectrum of mysterious stains. Still, it was the finest that the theatre had to offer and Dorian hardly ever noticed the décor these days. His eyes were only for Sibyl as she flowed onto the stage in a wispy light-blue dress that complemented her sculpted figure.

This night the play was *Much Ado About Nothing*. Sibyl portrayed an exuberant Beatrice with great zeal, delivering her lines with a subtle sensuality and playful wit that gave the audience no choice but to instantly adore her. The marvelous insight she showed while depicting the girl's vulnerability and weakness behind a jeweled mask of hardened sarcasm, was truly transformative. The audience showed their devotion to her and cried out again and again for an encore. Sibyl was happy to oblige them and was in her element, as she smiled gracefully and curtsied for the vigorously applauding crowd.

After the final curtain fell, Dorian slipped backstage and entered her modest dressing room silently, careful not to be seen by the actress. She was seated in an oval-backed chair that had seen better days. Her eyes were fixed on the cracked, but functional, wood-framed mirror as she slowly removed her colorful stage makeup. She barely caught sight of him from the corner of her eye, as he trailed his fingertips deftly from her delicate wrist and upwards, towards her collar bone which ended with a gentle caress of her porcelain cheek.

The contact warmed her to her core, and she was aghast at the tingling sensation it invoked between her thighs. She was unable to conceal the smile that his touch brought to her lips, or prevent herself from leaning back into his strong arms. Her head rested upon the firm chest muscles which were concealed beneath his plush waistcoat.

Ever the actress, a surprised look came over her face as she teased him. "A proper prince would announce his arrival and await an invitation before imposing himself so brazenly upon a lady in such a manner."

Dorian responded with a sly grin that hinted at future delights. "Your speech declares your annoyance, but your body begs for the second act to begin."

He tightened his biceps around her and squeezed firmly as his bold lips slowly brushed the pale curve of her slender neck with a feather-touch.

After a moment spent in silent enjoyment, she turned her head slightly to whisper seductively in his ear. "The second act is only the beginning. I have yet to bring you through many more delectable acts, each more pleasurable than the next—until at last, you reach the most satisfying climax of this play."

At that, he became immediately hard, his trousers growing taut, and Sibyl smiled wickedly as she felt the swelling against her thigh.

Dorian stepped back, suddenly at a loss for words, as his imagination danced across the various pleasures that her lithe form offered. A lustful haze fell over his eyes, and several seconds passed before his thoughts refocused and he regained his composure. He reached into his pocket and removed a delicately laced box. It was wrapped in an ornate, brightly-colored silk ribbon.

With a gallant bow, he offered her the treasure he cradled in his hands and heralded the gift with a husky voice. "A small trifle of my affection, my lady. It would honor me if you would wear it and accompany me to a gala to be held this evening by the Duke of Berwick."

With wide eyes and a gasp of delight, Sibyl received the fragile gift and tore into the soft packaging with alacrity. Her heart sang as she unwrapped the most beautiful golden and bejeweled necklace that her eyes had ever beheld. The gilded leaves of the cable were a delicate and ornate pure-gold. Set between them were rich flower petals with each of the metal blossoms holding a bud with a different shimmering stone. Clear, bright-white diamonds, deep-red rubies, brilliant-green emeralds, vivid-blue sapphires, and glistening topaz stones twinkled in the light. The necklace was in the style of some of her mother's finer costume jewelry pieces, but she knew this item to be assuredly authentic and exceedingly expensive. She began to cry at the generosity and beauty of such a lavish present.

Sibyl was breathless as she admired the necklace. "It is very lovely, but I couldn't possibly accept so extravagant of a gift. Besides, none of my dresses would be worthy to accompany it—or you, to such an elegant gala as the one held by the Duke."

Dorian laughed in a bright and conspiring way. "It is nothing compared to your beauty, my sweet—besides I have already dealt with the issue of the dress."

With that, he turned and opened the splintering door to the timeworn armoire that stood forlornly in the corner. He stepped to the side with a flourish to reveal a stunning gown that embodied the spirit of the necklace, hanging there expectantly. It was a soft-gold color as well, slim-fitting with a delicate cuirasse-bodice down to the thigh. The front and back of the dress dipped dangerously low in a provocative cut, with a sophisticated pattern of shimmering golden leaves offering the only modesty. The back of the dress was finished in an intricate train that flared wide and was complete with a fanciful network of glistening, inset stones. The entire gown was trimmed in vivid colors, which perfectly complimented the gems that were set in the necklace she had just received. It was truly a masterwork and the sizing and shape seemed like a perfect fit for her body.

"I had the seamstresses that make your stage costumes send the measurements to Paris—oof," he was cut off as Sibyl leapt into his arms, covering his face and neck with a fury of her passionate kisses. Her hands travelled experimentally across his chest and arms, before venturing lower towards his waist and stomach. Dorian grunted and backed into the wall behind him, returning her kisses with a fiery and desperate need. His hands found the curve of her waist and hips. Then he turned and spun her around, lightly forcing her backside against the wall. His fingers pressed lower, moving between Sibyl's slender thighs as his kisses descended between the swell of her supple breasts.

Suddenly, a knock at the door directly behind them rapped out a heavy beat. The door opened partially, and then immediately closed as the muffled voice of the theatre owner grunted out in a halting manner. "None o' that now, I lock up in a quarter hour. 'Tisn't proper—beggin' yo' pardon m'Lord. I'm not one ta interfere, but the other women in da troupe won't allow that sort a'thing—seein' as it's a shared dressin' room an' all. An' the girl's mother wo' be furious wi' me."

With a frustrated look, the couple untangled from each other's arms and tried unsuccessfully to smooth out their disheveled clothing. "One moment," Dorian called out in a commanding manner. He leaned into Sibyl's ear and spoke softly. "Change quickly and we'll be off. I'll distract him." With that, he exited the room and quickly closed the door behind him. Sibyl could hear his muffled voice as he attempted to stall the flustered owner with talk of remodeling the stage.

Sibyl hastily donned the golden dress and draped the glamorous necklace across her bustline reverently. She paused briefly to admire the way the jewelry curved with the swell of her bosom before fastening the golden clasps with the precision and speed of an actress long experienced in completing a complicated wardrobe change.

With a few minor touchups to her painted eyelids and long lashes, she finished the styling of her hair. It had, thankfully, been put up and pinned in a regal manner for her performance on stage only an hour earlier. With a discerning eye, she added a subtle kiss of paste and powder to complete the look. In a truly life-saving move one of the seamstresses had ostensibly sent her shoe size as well—for at the bottom of the armoire was a pair of delicate golden heels, embellished with gemstones and silk. Her stockings were serviceable, with the dress hopefully hiding the somewhat tarnished look of them. Pausing for one final glance at the mirror, she exited the room confidently.

Dorian was astonished and struggled to express his admiration as Sibyl emerged from her dressing room and into the hallway. "Good lord, you look exquisite—quite err, amazingly-dazzling." He was stunned by the beauty of this gorgeous creature. The owner could only stare in a state of awe, as Sibyl smoothly took Dorian's arm. He escorted her down the stairs, across the foyer and to the street where the carriage stood waiting to convey them to the gala.

CHAPTER 7.

THE DUKE'S GALA

The two were whisked away towards the wealthier side of town by a pair of swift, pure-black Friesian horses. They rode in a richly appointed four-wheel carriage with an enclosed cargo area and glass windows. While the carriage was in motion, Sibyl's reserve was once more tested as Dorian closed the curtains and began changing into a silk tuxedo with a tail coat. She couldn't quite bring herself to look away, as he teasingly removed his shirt and trousers and slowly put on the more elegant, white-silk shirt and midnight-black trousers. The two locked eyes briefly and an animal-like energy filled the space between them—ending only as Dorian completed his dress with a light, golden-silk vest and bow tie.

The homes they passed along the road grew more expansive and more elaborate until, finally, the carriage arrived at the steps of the grand house of the Duke of Berwick. A footman greeted the couple and assisted them as Dorian dashingly guided Sibyl from the conveyance. He kept his left hand firmly holding hers and his other upon the small of her back. They walked together and, after ascending the steps, the two were warmly received at the arching entryway. The iron double doors stood open and were lit with large, ornate lamps to greet the guests. As they walked through the halls, a series of cinnamon-colored mahogany doors opened instantly at their approach.   Finally, they were swept inside to the main ballroom along with the other arriving couples.

The stately ballroom was lavishly adorned with various rare artwork and exotic statues. A spattering of works that showed the proud face of the Duke or his fabled ancestors were spread among them. The eye was immediately drawn to the center of the room. There a flowing stonework peacock fountain shot water from its tail feathers and mouth. It was placed in the center of a gilded dance floor that had been constructed specifically for the evening. Brightly colored gas lamps highlighted the couples as they moved gracefully across the floor to intricately choreographed movements. Looking down upon the dancers was a tall ceiling which displayed baroque paintings in bright colors. The cross sections were adorned with sophisticated wood carvings and floral stonework. Several colossal crystal chandeliers hung low and spread a warm glow throughout the room.

The full orchestra was set to playing a lively waltz. With a laugh, Sibyl took Dorian's hand and pulled him towards the center of the floor. He smiled brightly as they assumed their positions with a bow. Dorian placed his right hand firmly on the back of Sibyl's left shoulder and pulled her close to him. The two began to move in unison as Dorian led with a confidence and boldness that put Sibyl at ease. She gazed deeply into his eyes as the two flowed across the floor. The music quickly diverged into various Polkas, Schottische, Valse à Deux Temps, and a modified Varsouvienne. Dorian's mastery of the many forms quickly put the other gentleman in attendance to shame. But all eyes were on Sibyl as she gracefully twirled and spun in her dazzling dress.

Throughout the evening, the pair were inseparable and remained together for nearly every song. They laughed together over private jokes and exchanged witty banter with the other guests. They drank sweet Champagne as they teased and flirted with each other late into the night. Finally, at half past twelve, a look of fear reached Sibyl's eyes as she realized the time. Dorian understood her plight immediately and escorted her without protest from the Duke's home to the waiting carriage. He instructed the driver to return to the poorer section where Sibyl's home was located.

During the carriage ride, Dorian and Sibyl sat very close and nestled together for warmth. Dorian lifted Sibyl's hand to his lips and planted several soft kisses on her palm and fingertips. He breathed softly as his mouth moved up to her delicate wrists. He paused at the sensitive skin of her inner elbow and let his tongue play, swirling around lightly. Sibyl let out a giggle of delight as the sensation both tickled and caused a throbbing between her thighs. Dorian continued to move upward, nibbling at her neck and shoulders while savoring the moment. Then, his lips began to explore her smooth face. When his mouth finally found hers, she opened her lips as their tongues darted in and out to intertwine in small circles. They caressed and stroked one another as the passion and heat grew—only to be interrupted by arriving at their destination far too quickly.

As the driver brought the carriage to a stop, Sibyl could barely bring herself to end the amorous and longing kisses the two now shared. She reluctantly urged Dorian to remain in the carriage, as she hurried out and towards the small apartment, where she knew her mother would be waiting—furious at the late hour of her return home.

Sibyl had to endure several multiple bouts of screaming and many threats to call the local constable to have her Prince Charming arrested before her mother finally calmed down. Eventually, the two women agreed to postpone the argument in favor of some much needed sleep.

The next morning, Sibyl tried to appeal to her mother's sense of romance and drama. "Mother, I am so happy." Sibyl sat with her mother, who was currently stooped over her sewing.

She sat in a faded armchair located in their dingy sitting-room. Mrs. Vane's thin figure seemed unjustly aged beyond her years. A hard life spoke of many bitter disappointments and relentless labor. This could be seen in her lined face, thinning straw hair, and dull eyes. Her wrinkled and cracked hands were no longer the smooth and powdered instruments of grace befitting an actress, but were now more suited to those of a scullery maid or seamstress. Yet, her nearly transparent and spotted skin was still framed around the delicate bone structure and heart-faced profile that had lent itself to her own long-gone acting career. Now that beauty could only be reflected in her only daughter.

"Happy?" Mrs. Vane winced at the ache in her hands as she struggled to pull the stubborn thread through the ever elusive eye of the needle. "I am only happy when I see you on stage. You mustn't let this Prince Charming of yours distract you from your acting. It is the death of a young thespian's career to fall for the wrong man. It happened to me, ruining my illustrious future on the stage and I won't have the same terrible fate befall you as well."

"Mother, what does acting matter when I have the affections of such a glorious young man? He is a gentleman and the kindest and most handsome man I have ever met!" Her lips parted with a remembered kiss and she trembled slightly, reliving the moments spent together as he had courted her.

Her Prince Charming had been shy at first, then surprisingly confident. His gentle demeanor gave way to more aggressive advances that bespoke of previous experience—but Sibyl didn't care. She loved him truly and deeply. "I love him, mother."

"Foolish child! It has only been a few weeks and you have only recently introduced him to me. I do not even know his rightful name! Rich he might be, but is he devoted to you? You must think of your acting above all things. Only with a firm offer of marriage should you even consider such a thing. Even then, a man's attentions can be a very fickle thing."

"Not my Prince Charming. He loves me as Antony did Cleopatra, as Orlando loved Rosalind! I do not even know why, or what I have done to deserve it. But he is the perfect image of what love should be. I know I am not worthy of him, but I try to be every day. Forgive me Mother, but I am so happy and I want to be this happy forever."

"You are far too young to fall in love. What do you really know of this man? Why, with your brother James leaving for Australia, this is a most improper time. Wait until your brother returns and can make the proper inquiries. How rich do you say he is? By his gifts, he certainly seems rich. Are you sure that necklace is real?"

The two broke off as the short, but stocky figure of James Vane entered the room. "Come Mother, Sister, it is time I was away—only first let me walk with Sibyl awhile to speak of this gentleman caller of hers."

"Ah James, my dear son, I will miss you dreadfully. How cruel the world is that we must be parted in such a way—but, I suppose, it must be so. You will return to us one day, with influence and position, to regale us with the great tales of your wonderful adventures. I hope you will be happy with your choice of a life at sea. You could have easily entered the troupe, or asserted yourself in London as a solicitor."

James patted her hand reassuringly. "Of course Mother. Only, promise me that you will watch out for Sibyl on my behalf. I hear this gentleman calls on her every night at the theatre."

"Oh James, do not worry. Of course I will watch over my own daughter. And this gentleman is very polite and obviously well connected. He is likely an aristocrat and if so it could be a brilliant match for your sister. He really looks remarkable and they make a most charming couple. They could contract a marriage alliance and he could fund her future performances— wouldn't it be glorious?"

Mrs. Vane glanced at her two children and with a grand theatrical gesture brought them both to her embrace. She played out the scene with tears brimming her eyes, as her children left her to make their farewells alone. It was a touching scene, worthy of one of her finer performances on the stage of her former life.

Her brother paced outside the small apartment in his impatient way. It was clear he was not fond of this subject of discussion. "Come, Sibyl."

The two exited the humble neighborhood and began strolling down the road near the park that framed the other meager surrounding buildings. It was a rough and poor area, but Sibyl felt confident with her brother's presence and safe walking under his protective gaze.

James pulled her aside. "Listen, I need to talk to you. When I am gone at sea there will be no one here to protect you. Who is this friend of yours you have been spending so much time with and staying out so late? It isn't right. Why haven't you told me about him? He is no good and will only hurt you. I don't even know his name!"

Sibyl grew angry and shouted. "Jim, stop! You must not speak anything against my Prince Charming. I love him!"

"How can you love him? You don't know anything about him."

"I know he is the most wonderful person in the world. You will meet him someday when you return from Australia. Then you will come to love him just as everyone else does. If only you would delay leaving for a few days and come to the theatre—he will be there and you two can meet. Then I will be Juliet, but for the first time actually in love."

"Beware of him Sibyl, I don't trust him. If he hurts you I swear I will kill him."

"Jim, don't talk that way. Some day you will be in love yourself and then you will know how I feel. Then you will understand. Life has been so terribly difficult for both of us but this is my chance. I have found the one to rescue me from it all and start a new adventure, just like the one you are setting out on."

"I suppose. As long as you truly love him."

"I will love him forever!"

"And he?"

"Forever, too!"

"He had better."

Sibyl merely smiled and put her hand on his arm. She led her brother to a lighted archway where they hailed an omnibus to take them home. Later, they parted in peace—save for the dangerous mistrust James held in his heart for this stranger who had come between the siblings. They said their emotional farewells and James made his way towards the misty docks and his thrilling new life at sea.

That evening, Sibyl met her Prince Charming at a darling little Italian Restaurant that had just opened. To Dorian, she had never seemed more exquisite. She was dressed in a simple but form-fitting blue dress, likely borrowed from the theatre for the occasion, and wearing the necklace he had gifted her. After she had discovered the engraving on the clasp: *for my dearest Sibyl Vane*, she hardly ever removed the piece of jewelry from her neck.

As the couple was seated at the candlelit table, they could hardly keep their hands from coming together under the table cloth. Dinner began with a brief caress here, and a lingering touch there. They started the meal with a very expensive-looking bottle of wine that Dorian selected. He expertly swirled the dark red wine in the sample glass that the waiter poured. As he raised the glass to his lips, an impish look appeared in his eyes. He leaned in for a kiss, and then secretively let some of the sweet liquid fall into Sibyl's ready mouth. "Do you find the wine satisfactory?"

She swallowed delicately and giggled. "Any wine delivered with such a kiss is more than satisfactory."

When the appetizers of buttered-kissed oysters with caviar arrived, Sibyl set to consuming hers in a seductive manner. She had Dorian's full attention, so she slipped off her shoe under the table and delicately ran her foot along the inside of his thigh. Dorian's oyster shot out of his hand and onto the floor. Sibyl laughed freely and spoke in a whispered voice. "Careful, they can get quite wet and slippery." Dorian was at a loss for words. Fortunately, the main course was arriving.

After a delicious dinner of pumpkin tortellini with grated cheese, the two shared a decadent pastry with chocolate filling. They fed the rich dessert to each other teasingly, placing a bite near the other's lips—only to pull it out of reach as the other bit down.

Then, after finishing more wine than was proper, Dorian paid the bill and bid the host to hail a hansom. He had the driver of the two-wheeled carriage take them on a romantic ride along the park. The moon brightened the night sky, preventing the couple from taking their kisses and fondling too far—for fear of the driver seated behind them seeing. It seemed to Sibyl, the most romantic evening of her life.

To her surprise, the hansom stopped at a private guest house Dorian had apparently rented for the evening. He dismissed her objections of impropriety and led her towards the arched entranceway. It was a beautifully appointed estate with an extensive garden out front. The grounds were filled with delicate smelling flowers, whimsical trees, small fountains, and beautiful statues. Sibyl was moved by the gesture and that Dorian would go to such a great expense. Perhaps it was the wine, but all objections faded on her lips when she looked into her love's eyes. They walked slowly through the garden, admiring the colors and scents and laughing together. The world began to fade until it contained only the couple, gazing longingly into each other's eyes. Upon entering the house, Sibyl was delighted to find the rooms adorned with all manner of flowers, delicate fruits, and an expensive bottle of Champagne.

Dorian removed the bottle from the ice, displaying it in his hands for Sibyl to admire. Sibyl rubbed the cork of the bottle suggestively. Dorian placed his hands over hers, and together they popped the cork. Sibyl gave a playful scream as she felt the small explosion. It crashed into the ceiling and the two laughed together again. He poured the frothy liquid carefully into a pair of delicate crystal flutes that were waiting on the table. Removing his coat, Dorian lifted his glass. "To a perfect evening with my beautiful love."

The two clinked their glasses together, maintaining a steamy eye contact. They each drank quickly, competing on who could finish the flute first. Dorian smiled knowingly as he let Sibyl win. He put down his glass, then grabbed her roughly about the waist. Sibyl gasped, as she felt a quiver of anticipation between her legs. Dorian leaned in but then pulled his kiss away, mimicking how he had teased her with the dessert earlier in the night. He clasped her hand with his and they danced slowly together, as if to some unheard music. The two drew ever closer and more intimate until Sibyl melted fully into his arms.

Dorian began kissing her neck, and she shivered as his lips brushed her skin. Dorian spun her in a simple twirl and Sibyl took flight, continuing her spin and whirling around as fast as she could—as she used to do as a child. She felt wonderfully dizzy.

Dorian chuckled and pantomimed her spin, then elegantly dropped to one knee. His face became suddenly serious, as he declared his undying love for her in a flowery prose that she was sure was borrowed from the work of some poet or another. Her heart leaped from her chest as he continued, looking deeply into her eyes. "We were destined to be together. Would you do me the honor of becoming my wife?"

The proposal must have been on a whim, for Dorian had no ring to offer, but Sibyl did not care. She loved him completely and the necklace was worth a dozen rings. Sibyl went to him, with tears in her eyes, and they embraced passionately. "Yes, yes, a thousand times yes! I love you with all my heart." The two stood together and began dancing again, this time in a mock-wedding waltz.

Dorian promised that after he requested the proper permission from her relatives, they would soon be engaged and he would let her pick out whatever ring she desired.

The two were so entranced, their minds so intermingled, it seemed they were already as man and wife. They danced slowly towards the bedroom door as if drawn by some magnetic force.

Dorian's hands became ever more daring as they deftly explored Sibyl's dress and the figure beneath. His fingertips snaked their way beneath the fabric to clasp her full breast and delicately trace along her soft skin down her backside. At his touch her skin tingled and a shudder of pleasure ran down her back, causing a pleasant moistness to arouse between her legs.

She pulled off his waistcoat, hastily breaking two of the buttons. She started to remove his silk shirt and trousers, her pulse quickening at the sight of Dorian's broad chest, strong shoulders, and taught muscles.

Dorian shed her dress skillfully and began removing her corset. They were both filled with an intense need as Dorian slowly kissed her full lips, perfect ears, and slender neck. His hands moved beneath her petticoat and found the swell of her exposed breasts, with his thumb gently flicking her hardened nipple. Then he moved his mouth to circle the other nipple with his tongue. Sibyl moaned in pleasure, as her hands struggled to release the swelling in his silk drawers.

Dorian suddenly lifted her off the ground in his powerful arms, causing Sibyl to gasp in surprise. He laid her down gently on the bed and the worship of her body continued, his tongue playing teasingly across the areola of her breasts, then to her taught waist and stomach, reaching her curvaceous hips, and finally exploring between her slender thighs.

Sibyl's chest and face flushed, as Dorian's tongue began to swirl around her clitoris. Finally, unable to wait any longer, she urgently pulled Dorian on top of her. The weight of his body felt so warm and reassuring.

Dorian groaned in pleasure as he finally entered her, thrusting slowly. The two became entangled in the most passionate moment that either had ever experienced. Time seemed to slow as they reveled in each other, Dorian grasping her hips and waist, and Sibyl scratching at his back and shoulders. Sibyl arched her back, and Dorian increased his pace, penetrating deeper as their need for one another crescendoed into the perfect climax.

Their muscles convulsed and they collapsed into each other's arms. The love-making had lasted longer than either could have hoped. They lay together, satisfied and intertwined in a most delicious exhaustion—all their senses tingling, at the perfect warmth and comfort they found in each other's bodies.

Later, as they quickly dressed, Dorian was filled with a most vicious, doubting regret. He vowed silently to correct this transgression and meet his gentleman's obligation, with the quick purchase of a ring and a formal proposal through Sibyl's mother. Until then, he swore her to a secrecy she agreed to most easily—as it was an incredibly romantic and dramatic thing, more vivid and forbidden than all the times she had played out the love between Romeo and Juliet on stage.

CHAPTER 8.

THE THEATRE

A week later, Lady Helena and Sage met with Dorian at the prescribed time. The three proceeded to the theatre with Dorian excited that his two friends would finally see Sibyl in all her glory and artistry as he had so many times before. As they were guided into his usual box, Dorian beamed with pride and anticipation. Finally, they would meet his lady love and see her for the brilliant actress that she was.

That night the house was as crowded as an overfilled barrel, its sides bursting with people. Laughter and voices filled the theatre with a discordant sound that made understanding each other quite difficult. Lady Helena was forced to raise her voice to be heard. "What a strange place to encounter a divine beauty that could capture your heart!"

Dorian re-examined their surroundings as if for the first time. "Oh, yes, it is a coarse and common place, but it is here that I found her. For even the finest gems are found among the rock and grit of the earth. How the crowd responds when she is on stage. They laugh and cry at her command and the audience is but her instrument, as the violin to the orchestra."

"Don't listen to her, Dorian," Sage intoned. "Any girl who can capture your heart must be marvelously talented and beautiful beyond description. If this Miss Vane of yours can truly make the common people forget the struggle of their lives but for a moment, if she can transcend selfishness and sorrow, if she can deliver beauty to their lives, then she is truly worthy of you."

The crowd hushed as the orchestra began to play. The great curtain, stained and threadbare in a few places, rose moments later. To thunderous applause, Sibyl Vane took the stage. She was certainly beautiful. In that moment Dorian was sure he was looking at one of the most hauntingly lovely creatures that he had ever seen. Sibyl made an apt Juliet as she took up the dance in the hall of the Capulet's house. Her body moved finely, with curves flowing like water, displaying an unworldly grace.

Despite that, her face seemed strangely distracted. Her eyes were listless and no joy could be found there. She seemed preoccupied as she scanned the crowd and delivered her lines strangely. Unlike her previous performances, her voice now carried an artificial tone. Her passion for her on-stage Romeo seemed forced and the inflection of her declarations of love rang hollow. Dorian grew puzzled and confused as he watched her cavort and frolic around the stage. His friends grew suddenly silent as if they dared not say a word. With horror, he began to sense their disappointment at Sibyl's performance and in her as his love interest. Dorian began to sweat. Perhaps she was ill—yes that was it. Undoubtedly some malady had befallen her, causing this result. There was something wrong but surely, surely her performance at the balcony scene in the second act would ring true. It was the climax of the play and any actress playing Juliet would certainly marshal her reserves for that scene.

Sibyl appeared on the tall balcony in the ivory moonlight. She looked the part perfectly. Her hair was adorned with a flowery wreath of the brightest flowers. Her figure was draped in delicate imported silk that matched the color of the moon. She was beautiful to behold. But again, her forced delivery was unbearably artificial and her gestures absurdly overemphasized. It was if she had been replaced by some school-girl understudy with imprecise emphasis and poor elocution. There was no meaning, no passion in her performance. It was a hollow and meaningless thing and simply bad art.

Even the uneducated paupers in the pit began to lose interest. They quickly became rowdy, talking and whispering amongst themselves and milling about. As the play progressed, harsh hissing and boorish laughter could be heard. The owner of the theatre swore and threw his cigar to the ground in disgust. Terror crept into Dorian's mind. Her performance was dreadful. How could this be happening?

Lady Helena gathered her things and put on her coat briskly, pausing to look Dorian straight in the eyes. "She is a beauty Mr. Gray—but she cannot act. Come let us go."

"I will see the play to its conclusion." Dorian's voice grew bitter. "I am sorry to have wasted your evening. I apologize profusely to you both."

Sage felt helpless. She tried to reassure him. "Dorian, I am quite sure Miss Vane was merely ill. She is certainly very beautiful. Perhaps we will come again on a different night when she is feeling better."

Dorian's voice shook and he appeared quite distraught. "I wish it was an illness, but it seems more than that. She has been entirely changed from the great artist I saw last week. This evening she is but mediocre and commonplace. Please leave me alone for tonight. I must think on this. My heart is completely broken." His face felt hot and flush with embarrassment, so he hid it with his hands and bowed his head.

Lady Helena tried to display some tenderness, but it only came off as pity. "There, there. Maybe the girl was simply nervous. Let us go to the club, Sage." The two swept out of the room together, leaving Dorian alone.

Dorian turned his pale face back towards the stage with a look of indifferent resolve. The play dragged on for what seemed an age. Half of the audience had left. The final act was greeted with nearly empty benches. The very moment the curtain fell, Dorian rushed backstage as quickly as he could. He burst into the back room to find Sibyl seated alone and looking at herself in a mirror. Upon seeing him in the mirror's reflection, her eyes lit with the fire of the sun and a golden radiance poured from her face. Her red lips smiled in a pouting way, as though with a hidden secret. All of the joy mysteriously absent from her performance suddenly flooded back into her gaze.

Sibyl laughed, apparently without any hint of the mortification Dorian keenly felt. "How badly I acted tonight, my Prince Charming."

"Horribly! Are you ill? You must tell me immediately and we will call for a physician. Why did you go on if you felt so poorly?"

Her smile faded slowly. "I suppose it is a form of illness, though not one that can be cured by any simple physician. It is the reason I was so bad tonight and why I will never act well again."

Dorian shook his head slowly from side to side. "Then you are ill. You should not perform in such a state. You make yourself and me seem ridiculous. I told you I was bringing my friends by this evening to see you. My friends were bored—I was bored. But what is this you mean by never acting well again?"

Sibyl didn't seem to be listening. She stared into his face

before speaking. "Before I knew you, acting was my whole life. It was the reason I lived and the meaning for getting out of bed every morning. I came alive in the many roles I played. The joys of Beatrice and the sorrows of Cordelia were my own. The scenes and the ever-changing stage were my entire world. But then you came into my world! My beautiful love, you freed my soul and you have become my whole life. You are the new reason that I now live. You have taught me what true joy is and that acting is but a hollow sham when compared to the grace and passion of our love. The pale moonlight on this dingy stage is false. The lines I deliver are not my own. They are but a reflection of the depths of reality."

Sibyl moved closer to Dorian until their faces were only a few inches away. "My Prince Charming! You are so much more than these small shadows of life. For the first time, I understood how perfect love can be. The hissing and boos of the audience meant less than nothing to me! Take me away with you, my Prince Charming. Take me away from this horrible stage where passion is but mimicked and affection is as ashes compared to the fiery heat of love burning for you."

Dorian flung himself back and turned his face away from her. "You have killed my love."

Sibyl looked at him unbelievingly and laughed with a nervous titter. She approached him again, touching his hair and grasping at his hand. Dorian drew away from her with a shudder.

His perfect, chiseled jaw hardened as he moved towards the door. "Yes, you have killed my love. It was your acting that stirred my imagination, but now you do not even stir my curiosity. I loved you because you were exceptional. It was your genius while acting on the stage and because you shared my dreams of the great poets of our time. You gave shape to the substance of their art. Now you have thrown it all away. How stupid and shallow of you."

His face turned into a scowl and his eyes flashed with anger. "My God! What a fool I was to love you! How mad I must have been. You are nothing to me now and I will never see you again. Nor will I think of you, or ever mention you again. I wish I had never laid eyes upon your accursed face. I would have made you famous and the world would have worshipped you. You would even have borne my name in time. Now you will be nothing more than a third-rate actress with a pretty face."

She trembled and turned a chalky shade of white. "You are not serious? You can't be. It is an act. Tell me this is all an act."

His tone became sarcastic and his face filled with a bitter grimace. "Acting! Ha, I leave that to you since you do it so well."

A look of sharp pain entered her face and she reached out to him while gazing searchingly into his eyes. But he only thrust her back. "Don't touch me!"

A straggled moan escaped her delicate throat and she

wilted to the floor like a trampled flower. "No! Don't leave me. I am sorry I didn't act well. I was only thinking of you the whole time. I will try. Yes, I will do better. I can remember a time before we kissed, before we—came together as one. Kiss me again my love. We are engaged remember? We were to announce the news to everyone. You mustn't leave me. I couldn't bear it. Can't you just forgive me for tonight's mistake? I will work hard to improve and do whatever you say. Please do not be so cruel, I love you more than anything in the world. This is the first time I haven't pleased you. It was foolish and I couldn't help it. Just don't leave me, please don't leave me." Her pleas became inaudible with a sobbing that choked off her voice.

Dorian looked down at her as she crouched on the floor and saw only a wounded creature, like a pitiful wolf cub. But instead of compassion or pity, his perfect lips curled upward into a look of disdain. How absurdly melodramatic and annoying her flowing tears and hiccupping sobs were to him. How had he ever loved a woman such as this? He had ceased to love her entirely.

His voice was unbearably calm and even. "I am going. I can no longer see you anymore. You have disappointed me."

She continued to weep as she stretched her hands out to him imploringly, but made no other reply. Dorian turned sharply on his heel and strode quickly from the room and out of the theatre forever.

When he arrived home, Dorian went straight to his Library to pen a note of apology for wasting the time of Lady Helena and Sage. As he sat down to write, he paused to look at his portrait which he had hung on the wall. His face was full of joy and beauty as ever. With a start, he looked at the wolf cub. It must be his imagination. The wolf seemed much older than the cub had been when it was painted. The eyes were too cunning and the face smiled at him disdainfully. Impossible. He disregarded the thought and bent to compose his letter.

CHAPTER 9.

THE WOLF

Early the next morning, Dorian called upon Sage at her home. Their visits had grown less frequent as of late, but now he sought to rekindle their friendship in order to take his mind off of recent events. The wolf had thrived and was now nearly to adulthood. Ample food and exercise had filled out the wolf and added strong muscles spread beneath the shiny gray coat. A new look of intelligence and cunning had replaced the once innocent and playful face. Although significantly larger, the animal still took cuts of meat straight from Dorian's hand. Sage had cared for the wolf for most of its life and he usually took meat from her hand as well, but today the offer was met with a stark refusal. The privilege now seemed reserved only for Dorian.

Sage once again attempted to feed the wolf a small choice cut of beef from her proffered hand. "Dorian, why doesn't he like me?"

"I am sure he likes you just find my dear. He owes you so much, but perhaps he is just tired of you forcing your attentions on him in such a manner."

"Where did my little, baby wolf cub go? How did my tiny *Dorian Grey* grow up so fast?"

For the briefest of moments, Dorian was offended—until he remembered that Sage insisted on referring to the beast as his namesake.

"That is the very problem, Sage. You treat him still as the young lapdog that he was, instead of the dangerous predator he has become. Maybe if you coddled him less, he would respond to you more."

"Dangerous? Why, no one holding the name Dorian could ever be dangerous to anyone," said Sage as she reached one hand towards the wolf's ear and the other hand again offered up the bloody piece of meat towards the sharp teeth.

As if to refute her statement, at that very moment the wolf snarled and snapped at the beef with needlelike teeth. His teeth sunk into the meat along with the more delicate flesh of Sage's hand.

She cried out and quickly pulled the hand back. "RaaAhh! How could you do such a thing?"

Dorian rushed to her side. Already both the tears from her face and blood from her hand were falling. Together they splattered on the floor. He laughed merrily as he started to inspect the wound. "It is but a small hurt, likely to leave only a minor scar. You should have listened to me." He began to clean the wound as Sage's shock grew along with the pain in her palm and fingers.

"My brush-hand! Oh you wretched beast. Perhaps you do need to be free of me and out in the world. Out! Out I say!"

The wolf had not the decency to look reproached, but instead his eyes gleamed with ferocity and his lips curled up to revel the sharp teeth along with a bloody muzzle. For a moment, it seemed like he might snarl again or even bare his teeth further. Then the animal turned quickly, without so-much-as a backward glance, and bounded across the room and towards the open door.

"*Dorian Grey* wait! Don't leave me like this." Sage struggled to rise from the floor, between tears and a hand slick with blood. She pressed the puncture marks closed on her hand in an attempt to stop the bleeding.

Instead of slowing however, the wolf increased his pace from the house and bounded towards the forest. He sensed the need for freedom beating in his heart. The bloodlust to kill live prey was growing inside of him and he longed for the thrill of the hunt.

Later that evening, after Sage had been soothed and her hand tended to, Dorian strode from the house and out into the night. He moved towards the ancient, gnarled trees of the darkened forest. His vision was actually quite good in the poor light, aided of course by the bright stars and the waxing moon.

How foolish he had once been, to be afraid of the unknown. How childish he had been to fear imagined monsters lurking behind the ancient statues of wood. How naïve he had once been in avoiding the night and all of its wondrous delights.

As he walked on along the border of the thick shadowy-wood, he suddenly knew that he was no longer alone. "So, you still know who your master is and who it was that saved you years ago from certain death?"

The wolf whined in response to Dorian's outstretched hand, quickly covering the distance between the two figures. The animal sat submissively and began panting with an expression of utter devotion. Dorian's fingers luxuriously scratched out a pattern behind his ears and along his head. In Dorian's presence the animal was completely tame and obedient. It knew instinctively who was the pack leader and the Alpha male. There was a type of kinship between the two. It was an instinctual understanding about the need for freedom, the thirst for new experiences, and the desire for fresh prey.

"Off you go. Time to enjoy these prime years of your life far away from the destructive hand of mankind. Better not to be tethered to one such as Sage Holdsworth, when there is so much more that awaits you in the green forest."

With a flick of his wrist, Dorian dismissed the wolf and it ran off into the darkness. Dorian knew that whenever he walked the edge of the dark forest in the future, the beast could be summoned back to him with the ease of a low whistle. In the days that followed, whenever the wolf caught wind of his pack leader's scent on the air, he would cover the ground quickly in order to be nearby. There he would lurk at the tangled edges of the forest in the blackness, in case he was ever to be summoned by the Master.

The wolf grew stronger and more confident as time passed in his new domain. He also grew more vicious, much more cunning, and more accustomed to the darkness in his new realm. He learned to avoid detection as he moved about the ancient woods. His first hunt was triggered by the scent of a young fawn that was separated from her mother.

The small, fallow fawn had wandered into a clearing deep in the forest. Its coat was chestnut with pale spots that ended in a white tale with a black stripe. It was only a few weeks old, but already the large eyes were cautious as it moved around on unsteady feet.

The wolf gradually stalked his prey, remaining completely unnoticed at first. While repeatedly tasting the air, the slim animal finally sensed the danger. The scent of the young fawn grew thick with fear. The wolf savored the anticipation, the energy of a young fawn's life, and relished the moment when he finally leapt out and into the view of the budding fawn. It shook in terror and turned to run. It was all too easy for the wolf to overtake the young animal and enthusiastically sink his sharp teeth into her slender neck. With a twist of his jaws he broke the neck. As the hot blood rushed into his mouth, the wolf sank to the forest floor and began to devour his kill.

Several days passed as the wolf explored his growing territory. There was no competition for prey here, nor threat from any other large predators. Live food was a vast improvement over the cold, dull cutlets the wolf was used to receiving. He would never go back to that.

The next hunt brought the wolf upon a juvenile Red deer that was grazing peacefully in a pristine field. The hind was much larger. It was close to two hundred centimeters in length and weighing near one hundred and fifty kilograms. Her hide was a reddish hue and she had a long tail. The doe was really quite beautiful as she grazed daintily among tall grasses and bushes. The wolf's pulse quickened at her scent, and his mouth salivated when he caught sight of the delicate neck.

This time the hunt involved a great deal more sneaking and hiding behind shrubs and bushes. The adult female was much more observant and experienced. She caught wind of the attack much sooner which resulted in a large amount of running through the dark woods. This, too, was a new and exciting form of danger for the wolf. He toyed with his prey, closing in on her and then falling back to give the illusion of hope for escape. For what seemed like hours, he pursued the doe and then drew back. It was a dance between two lovers in the night, a most delicious game.

At last, as the doe's heart began hammering to the point

of ripping out of her chest, she became cornered against a massive cave wall. Though she was frantic with the need to escape, the wolf blocked her path to freedom and descended slowly. He was careful so as not to lose the opportunity to strike. He lashed out with sharp claws and greedy fangs, tasting her hot blood. Again and again he struck, prolonging the moment of the kill. At last, he used his sharp teeth to hamstring the animal. He leaped upon her back and used his weight to drive the thrashing animal to the ground. She was no longer able to run. He began devouring her while she was still alive at his feet.

The wolf grew bolder and increasingly unafraid of his surroundings. He was less wary of man, and more confident than ever in his newfound abilities. All of the night was his domain. He was king of the trees and the fields and the rivers. He even dared to enter the forbidden areas at the edges of the forest. There he stole unsuspecting young chickens and unwary female calves from the pathetic defenses and not-so-watchful eyes of their human protectors.

Dorian too, grew bolder in his exploration of the pleasures of the world. He became enamored with the thrill of his own hunt. It was not uncommon, to see him entertaining a different young lady every night. His territory was the various theatres and balls thrown across town. At any dinner party, he was always the center of attention for the young ladies. He charmed them easily with his exceptional looks and meticulous style. His growing popularity could be attributed to his unending confidence, mischievous wit, and copious wealth. He was playful and debonair, gallant and wicked—and the women loved him for it.

At a particularly large gala in the city, Lady Helena was introduced to not one—but two entirely different young ladies. Both were clearly infatuated with Mr. Gray's charming good looks, gaudy and stylish displays of fortune, and blossoming popularity in society. They were both quite nubile and voluptuous.

The first was a comely blonde of some good standing. Her lips were full and pink, with startling blue eyes and a generous bust. She caught the attention of every young gentleman in attendance.

The second was a winsome brunette with the dark, deep eyes of a doe. She was visiting her family from their country estate and had developed her own following of admirers. She was the very image of feminine perfection, with perfectly proportioned curves and long, slender legs.

To Lady Helena however, they were too similar to tell apart. They even wore a similar shade of pink evening dress that was currently in favor. Neither of the long gowns left much to the imagination, given the tight fit and plunging necklines.

The evening became increasingly dangerous. Dorian would spend a few moments drinking a cocktail with one at the bar, then move near the dance floor and begin laughing audaciously with the other. He would carry on the conversation with that one for a few moments before switching back. It became clear that both girls thought themselves wholly the sole target of his affections. They were completely oblivious as Dorian repeatedly excused himself for one reason or another—in the most polite manner, of course. Both girls remained ignorant to the whispers and stares as Dorian whisked them in-turn across the elongated dance floor, in perfect time to the tune of the orchestra.

Lady Helena was amazed how ignorant the two were to the entire charade. Instead of seeing what was happening, the girls busied themselves by basking in the attention of the crowd. They misinterpreted the scrutiny as appreciation and jealousy. Lady Helena thought it all a tremendous comedy. She was quite accommodating in drawing one of them away as Dorian danced and flirted with the other.

Even the smirk on Lady Helena's face did not clue them into the other girl's presence until, at last, Dorian became increasingly bold and reckless for he was delighted to see what would happen, and how far he could push the envelope during the course of the evening. Finally, the blonde caught site of Dorian stealing a kiss from the brunette and stormed across the dance floor to pull him aside and express her outrage.

She had a genuine look of hurt in her dazzling eyes, as she dumped what remained of her drink on Dorian's waistcoat. "How could you?"

Without any regard to his dampened attire, he lied smoothly and convincingly in response. "My dear, it is nothing. A mere dalliance and an effect of the wine, I assure you. Come, let me take you home and make it up to you."

She almost fell for the ploy. The promise of winning such a prize as Dorian Gray nearly overruling her better judgment. The conflict could be seen playing out behind her stunning blue eyes. The prospect was tempting, but she had suffered too much shame that evening. Her pride compelled her to storm out of the room. She paused briefly with a backward glance and a warning for the brunette—delivered with pouty and moistened lips. "You would do well to find better company, and acquaint yourself with a *real* gentleman rather than this philanderer. I didn't believe the rumors about him, but now I see that they are altogether true. You would be wise to take heed of them as well."

The vivacious brunette had the gleam of victory in her glittering eyes. She was certain that this rejected competitor was merely jealous of her beauty and the warning was disregarded as bitterness from such a stinging loss. Perhaps she had indulged in too much wine as well, for she thought the result her good fortune. She offered no resistance, as Dorian escorted her out of the hall and into a waiting hansom.

The entire scene was quickly recounted, time and time again, and the rumor of it spread like wildfire among the social elites. The tale only served to add to the mystery and notoriety already being spread about the remarkable Dorian Gray.

CHAPTER *10.*

THE CHANGE

It was nearly dark. The wolf had been resting in his makeshift den, deep in the heart of Epping Forest. Gnawed bones and discarded antlers littered the surrounding ground. A nearby stream provided a ready supply of water. He had carefully marked all of the surrounding trees with his scent to ward off any intruders

The wolf had grown in size and intelligence. So he had both the need and the means to dig out the small hollow where he now made his home. It was a safe spot and difficult to find, sheltered by mossy-green rocks and fallen tree trunks from the unpleasant rain and persistent cold. The wolf sat upright, while he used his powerful claws to move away large boulders and stones.

The paws that held the claws had become larger and more dexterous. The due claw was now separated and bending outwards while also growing longer. This allowed the wolf to grasp ahold of the variously-sized rocks and move them with surprising accuracy. With the bare earth exposed, the wolf used his powerful hind legs to dig out enough room for his enlarged shoulders and widened torso. These could fit comfortably inside while concealing his entire body from sight. Not that any animals were foolish enough to come close to the wolf's den. He remembered when he had taken the territory from a large brown bear that had likely escaped from a nearby bear-baiting pit.

The large predator was covered in battle scars from dozens of fights with vicious Bulldogs which were starved until they were ravenous. The bear was strong and confident in his ability to defend his territory. As the wolf approached it, the enormous creature reared up on powerful hind legs. The bear must have weighed over five hundred kilograms and was nearly three meters in height. The wolf snarled his challenge and began to circle the large creature wearily. The bear was unimpressed. There was no scaring him off. This confrontation would be to the death.

As he began his assault, the wolf relied on his superior speed to keep the massive animal off balance. He lunged in to strike at the bear's legs and stomach with claws and teeth, then dodged away as the massive paw descended in answer. The creature roared as the wolf bloodied it, frustrated that it could not strike the wolf in return. The wolf continued to attack until the enraged animal finally surged forward, falling onto all fours. In a burst of speed, the full bulk of the bear slammed into the wolf and sent him sprawling backwards.

The wolf had barely any time to recover before the bear's claws raked across his back and side. The immense animal was too close to evade, so the wolf rose up on his hind legs. This gave his front claws the freedom to sink deep into the bear's shoulders and neck. The bear rose up to his full height again and the two traded blows back and forth, dealing devastating injuries to each other.

The wolf was outmatched, but he refused to give up. Suddenly, the bear's left leg buckled as the bloody ruin was no longer able to support the immense weight. The huge animal began to fall. In a burst of urgency, the wolf pushed sideways and narrowly avoiding being crushed beneath it. Seeing his chance, the wolf leapt onto the back of the bear and sunk his teeth into the muscular neck as deeply as possible. Blood poured out, but the wolf had not severed the artery. The bear wasn't finished yet. Massive shoulders tried to roll the wolf off, as huge claws scored deep gashes in the wolf's flanks. The bear rose from the ground and began thrashing in every direction in an attempt to throw the wolf off. To allow that would mean death for the wolf and so he clamped down with all his might. He desperately sunk all of his claws into the heavy hide. Gradually, the thrashing beneath him slowed. The bear tried to run but was dazed from blood loss and crashed into the surrounding trees and rocks. Finally, with a groan of anguish, the warrior bear sank to the ground and surrendered to the warm embrace of death.

It had taken many days for the grievous wounds inflicted by the bear to heal. He was unable to hunt and would surely have starved if not for the ready supply of meat that the gigantic carcass provided. Once he was healed, the wolf returned to hunting the smaller deer among the trees. Still tender from his scars, the wolf sometimes sought out easier prey. He was fast becoming an expert at killing the fat Suffolk sheep that lived in the small villages lining the outskirts of the forest.

The trick with the black-faced sheep was to approach the nervous animals slowly from downwind—ideally while they were sleeping. The wolf would leap over any small wooden fences that protected the flock. Then he would rush into the fleecy group while they were still unaware of his presence. It was best to kill a few as quickly as possible and carry one off. That way he could be gone before they set to their incessant bleating. Sometimes, the noises would alert a sheepdog that would rush in and begin barking his challenge to the vastly bigger wolf. The annoying animals were foolish to test the dominance of the wolf. He would quickly dispatch any dogs with a few swipes of his powerful claws, or by pinning the animal down and ripping out its throat. He had learned a painful lesson to flee, however, whenever the farmers themselves exited their homes. They would frequently brandish a Brunswick percussion rifle or Baker muzzle-loading rifle that the wolf had come to think of as a "fire stick."

The first time he had been hit by one of the small lead balls, he had been feasting on several sheep in an enclosed field. He was gorging himself on their blood and innards, and so had missed the approach of the accursed farmer in the midnight darkness. The burning pain had hit the wolf, almost simultaneously as the flash of fire and terrifying smell of smoke registered to his senses. He had yelped loudly and instantly abandoned his kill to flee for the protection of the trees. Loud bangs had followed him on his flight and another of the terrible balls had grazed his ear as he leaped the final outer fence. The fire-ball had lodged itself deeply in the wolf's shoulder. Pulling the vile object out with his claws proved even more painful than when it had struck him. He had licked the wound constantly and now knew to be more watchful. Since that day he had avoided man more carefully. Eventually, the lack of game in the forest caused the hunger to return and drove the wolf to enter the villages again.

It was pitch black as the wolf waited along the outskirts of the small village. He would rest here often, completely hidden as he listened to the oblivious men speak to each other. At this hour the men had long since gone to bed, but the danger of their fire-sticks was always present. If he made too much noise they would pour out of their homes like fire ants.

The wolf avoided all areas of light or movement and tested the air carefully before proceeding forward. The farmers had taken to hiding their livestock in the large barns at night. The wolf hated to approach so closely to any of the buildings, but he could almost taste the blood of the animals inside. He would need to do this carefully. He approached the smallest of the buildings that was also the most isolated. The split-level barn smelled strongly of grain. Three of the walls were built from stone. The front wall, however, contained two large doors for a wagon to pass through and was made entirely from wood. That would be his way in.

As he approached, he caught a whiff of the large, four-legged animals that the men called "horses." It was becoming easier to understand the men when they talked about the animals they labored to feed and protect. Lately, many of those words had begun to make sense to the wolf. It was different than when he interacted with the Master. That was more instinctual, more of the wordless communication between members of the pack. The sounds that the other men formed were difficult to separate and understand, but the wolf was learning.

The barn door was closed and barred by a heavy beam that had taken four men to put in place. Careful not to make a sound, the wolf grasped the mass of wood and lifted it clear. The action caused only soft scraping noises and a dull thump as he dropped the timber on the grassy ground. Then he silently lowered himself to all fours and nosed open the door. The wolf paused to listen. He heard the even breathing of a horse in the corner stall of the barn. He could smell no other creatures inside, save for a few small rats and the ever-present dung insects.

The wolf entered the barn as quietly as possible and padded across the hay-strewn floor. He began to stalk the chestnut-colored stallion that was asleep in the stall. It was a large animal, with powerful hooves and sharp teeth that the wolf had acutely learned to avoid. They were very difficult animals to take down when out in the open. Horses had often eluded him, detecting his scent and running away at a high speed. If he did get close to one it would lash out with tenacious defenses to deliver stunning bruises and deep lacerations—that the wolf remembered all too well. But this horse had nowhere to flee to and no warning of his approach.

The wolf was nearly ready to spring, carefully positioning himself between the stall and the open door of the barn. The nostrils of the horse flared and the white of his eyes widened in alarm. He had been discovered. The wolf lunged at the horse with open jaws. The horse moved quickly, spinning and kicking. At the last instant, the wolf was able to twist his body to avoid the kick, but at the cost of slamming head first into the stone wall of the barn. He was dazed momentarily as the horse reared and began stamping and kicking wildly. Shaking his head to clear it, the wolf scrambled, trying to avoid the deadly assault. The hooves slammed into the wolf's tail and leg. Blinding pain shot through him. Rage filled the wolf. How dare his prey challenge him?

He struck out with knife-like claws to destroy the offending horse leg. Rising to his hind legs, the wolf grappled with the stallion and began pushing it against the side of the stall. The horse screamed and foamed at the mouth as it struggled to escape, but the wolf pinned it stubbornly in place. He ignored the superficial bites and inflicted deeper ones into the exposed flank of the horse. The wooden stall cracked and splintered, giving way under the tremendous weight of the two animals.

With straining muscles, the wolf partially lifted the horse as they fell. He was able to tilt the heavy frame and land on top of the animal with a thunderous crash. The stallion thrashed on the ground desperately trying to rise, but the wolf ignored the injuries he had received and closed his jaws on the carotid artery of his prey. For long minutes, he held the neck of the horse down as it slowly died. His claws opened the warm stomach and chest of the animal, and he released his hold to consume the still beating heart.

The farmers burst in through the door a moment later. The light from their lanterns illuminated the damage done to the stall and the blood-spattered carcass of the stallion. They brought their fire-sticks to bear, but there was nothing else in the stall. The wolf had leaped straight upwards and he now clung to the rafters with a large beam supporting the weight of his legs. As the men approached the stall they did not immediately think to look up.

The wolf saw his way out through the trap door to the second loft above. He readied his muscles for the jump. The men finally raised their lights and pointed their weapons upward.

Before he could be exposed, the wolf crashed through the trap door. He raced along the threshing floor and smashed through the loft doors to fall two stories to the ground below. Shots of lead balls rang out just behind him as he made his frantic escape. The wolf sprinted back to the cover of the forest as the alarm was raised throughout the village.

CHAPTER 11.

DARK RUMORS

It was long past noon when Dorian finally awoke in his bedchamber. His valet had crept upstairs and into the room several times to see if his master had yet begun to stir. He wondered what made him sleep late so often. Finally, the bell rang and the valet entered with a pot of strong black tea, a selection of fine bacon and delicate sausage, the day's correspondence, and yesterday's edition of *The Globe*. All these were served meticulously on an ancient set of light-blue china.

The valet gave Dorian a cautious smile. "Monsieur has slept well this morning?"

Dorian let loose a lazy yawn as he stretched his neck and shoulders. "I suppose so. What o'clock is it, my good man?"

"One hour and a quarter, Monsieur."

So late! Dorian sat up slowly and began sipping his tea while turning over his letters. How interesting. One had been hand delivered that morning from Lady Helena. He put that one aside for the moment and instead began opening the usual tedious dinner invitations, routine tickets to private shows, mundane charity programs, and other of the like that were constantly showered on fashionable young men of his caliber.

One letter in particular contained a heavy bill for a fanciful, chased silver Louis-Quinze toilet. The common people simply did not realize that unnecessary things are the only real necessities in life. The rest of the letters all contained very elegant and courteous communications from several Jermyn Street money-lenders, each offering to advance Dorian large sums of money—for the most reasonable of interest rates and at a moment's notice.

After dressing in a new pair of silk trousers, he took the letter from Lady Helena to the library to continue his breakfast. As his valet slunk out of the room, his eye happened to track across the portrait that Sage had painted of him and the wolf cub. Dorian shook his head as if to clear his vision. Surely there was still some drowsiness in his eyes. He blinked rapidly and moved closer to the painting. Did the portrait look different? Was it his imagination, or was something terribly off about it?

The image of Dorian himself had not altered, of course. It was the same chiseled face of timeless beauty as always. But the image of the wolf cub had changed in a most impossible way. The wolf in the painting had become larger—much larger. Larger, and more terrifying! The eyes were filled will malice and rage. They shone with a bloodlust and intellect that was unnatural. It far surpassed the normal look of any deadly predator. The beast's coat had become a much darker grey and no longer had a healthy sheen to it, but rather a mangy and sickly look. The wolf's face too had changed substantially. The massive teeth had now become more pronounced and extended from the squared, yet somehow more human-looking jaw. In fact, the entire animal had changed in proportion and shape to take on a more elongated and bipedal appearance.

That was completely absurd. A painting could not alter! But what if it was true and reflected a real change of the wolf's appearance? How long had it been since he had really seen how his wolf looked outside the cover of the shadows of the forest? Surely, it could not resemble this hideous creature before him. Yes, the painting had altered. That was a fact.

He gazed at the image with a growing sense of horror. The cruelty of the beast made him think of how cruel he had been to Sibyl Vane, how predatorily he had acted towards the other young ladies that he had hunted through the recent nights. A deep sense of guilt began to cloud his mind. Maybe it was not too late for him to change his ways. Maybe this strange picture was a warning sent through the magical brush of dear Sage. Perhaps it was meant to somehow guide him through life and transform him back into a more noble and unselfish version of himself. He recalled all of the illicit nights of sin. His mind was filled with memories of intoxication from the heavy drinking and the use of questionable stimulants. Like a flash, he relived all the instances of intense debauchery. His mind was flooded with a feeling of remorse, which he had strangely never felt before. It was as if this painting had become a visible symbol of the degradation of his soul, but visited instead upon an innocent and helpless animal.

The hour struck three and then four, but still Dorian did not stir. He was too deep in contemplation and the study of his own profound sorrows and copious passions. His mind languished through a labyrinth of conflicting shame, entangled needs, and shifting desires. Finally, not knowing what else to do, Dorian sat at his writing table and penned out a passionate letter to Sibyl.

She was the girl he had once loved with his entire mind and body and he desperately implored her forgiveness while decrying his own selfish madness. Yes, he would set things right once more and begin again fresh. He would correct his path and return to the point where his life had deviated from the righteous course of a Godly and holy man. He would immediately marry Sibyl and all would be set right.

There is a true luxury in self-reproach. We can blame ourselves more thoroughly and imaginatively than any other can. It is surely the confession and resolve to change that provides the absolution, as much as the simple priest behind the lacquered screen.

A demanding knock at the door interrupted his thoughts. He heard Lady Helena's voice outside. "Mr. Gray, I must see you at once. It is most urgent."

The knocking continued and quickened when Dorian made no immediate answer. Perhaps, it was better to let Lady Helena in and explain the important changes he would be making to his life, even if it meant the two would have to part ways. Better not to delay the change of direction in his life or the hurt it would cause to his dear friend. He quickly threw the screen across the picture and rose to unlock the door.

Lady Helena hurriedly entered the room with a worried look on her face. "I am so sorry for it all, Dorian. Try not to dwell on it too long."

"Do you mean about Sibyl Vane?" he asked in an absent-minded way.

Lady Helena gracefully lowered herself into a chair and removed her white, kidskin gloves. Her reply was biting. "Yes, of course. The incident was really quite dreadful, but entirely none of your doing. Tell me, when you ended things with the ill-fated girl—did you make much of a scene?"

"I was a savage, my dear, really quite barbarous. But now I will set all to right. I do not, however, regret anything that has happened. It has taught me so much about myself."

"Good for you. I am glad to hear that you are taking this mishap in stride! I was fearful you would be in a deep despair. That would ruin the complexion of that marvelous face of yours."

A cautious smile reached his lips. "I have gone through

that. I assure you, I am perfectly happy now. For the first time I truly understand what it means to have a conscience. The experience is not at all how you describe it, but something divine. I desperately want to be honorable and repair the damage that I have done. I can't stand the idea of my soul becoming a lecherous and grotesque thing."

"What a charming take on ethics you have. But how will you begin this miraculous transformation?"

"By marrying Sibyl Vane."

"Marrying!" bellowed Lady Helena as she stood to gaze at him in astonishment. "But, my dear Mr. Gray...did you not receive my letter?
I wrote you only this morning and sent the note by my own man.

"Your letter? Oh, yes, I remember it now. No I haven't read it yet. Why? Was there something urgent written inside it?"

"So you don't know?"

"Know what Lady Helena?"

Lady Helena crossed the room and took Dorian's hands in her own. As the two sat, her grip tightened ever so slightly.

She searched his eyes. "Dorian, don't be frightened—my letter—was to tell you that Sibyl Vane is dead."

A cry sprang unbidden from Dorian's mouth as he jumped to his feet and flung Lady Helena's hands down. "Dead! Sibyl dead? That is a terrible lie and not true! How could you say such a thing?"

Lady Helena's voice was grave. "I'm afraid it is quite true. It is spread across all the morning papers. I wrote to you about it and to ask that you speak to no one until we had a chance to meet. There will be an inquest, of course, and you must not be mentioned when questions arise."

She leaned in closer and placed her hand on Dorian's knee. "Things like this can be fashionable in Paris, but in London the society here is really quite prejudiced. One should never have their debut clouded with scandal or dark rumors. Those things should come with old age. I suppose they do not know your name at the theatre? Tell me, did anyone see you visit her in her room?"

Dorian was unable to answer for several moments. When he was able to speak it was difficult to get the words out. "Did—did you say there was to be an inquest? What do you mean by that? Be quick, and tell me everything at once."

"It really is quite curious and most horrific. It seems that as the girl was leaving the theatre in the evening at about half-past twelve, she decided to walk by the park in her neighborhood. There she was set upon by Jack the Ripper. Either that fiend or the High Rip Gang assisted by some Bulldogs—the constables are still debating various theories. They found her body dragged to the middle of the park. It was absolutely ripped apart you see. She met quite a brutal end with slashes and cuts everywhere and her throat and intestines torn out. She was so badly mutilated, the coroner was only able to identify the body by the engraving on the necklace she wore which bore her name."

"Stop, please stop! I can't bear to hear anymore, how terrible!"

"Yes it is very tragic. Things are quite out of control in the poorer areas of the city. Something really must be done about it. There have been several vicious attacks and murders of the like in recent weeks. But you must not get yourself mixed up in it all. I see by *The Standard* that the poor girl was seventeen. She seemed even younger, looking like such a child as she did—and with so little acting ability. But, you mustn't let this trouble you. Come and dine with me this evening, and afterwards we will go to the opera."

Dorian spoke in a hushed tone. "So, I have murdered Sibyl Vane. Murdered her as surely as if I had cut her pretty little throat myself. This is a tragedy. It is too late now to go back and fix things to how we were before. Oh, if only I had not been so cruel to her! If only I had never walked into that theatre and never seen her upon the stage!"

He looked out the window just then and continued. "Yet somehow, the birds still sing merrily in the garden. The crimson roses are no less lovely or fragrant. Tonight we will dine together on some delicacy and see art performed at the opera. How extraordinarily dramatic life is! Lady Helena, if I had read this in a book I would weep for days. Somehow, with it actually happening to me it seems too full of wonder for tears. There on my desk is the first passionate love-letter which I have ever composed in my life—and it is addressed to a dead girl. Can the dead feel, I wonder? Can Sibyl know now, that I meant to come back to her? How I deeply loved her once. She was everything to me! I said I would go back to her and now she is dead. My God. What shall I do? I might be in danger! She had no right to get herself killed. It was quite selfish indeed."

Lady Helena removed a cigarette from her gold-leafed case and struck a match. "My dear Mr. Gray, if you had married this girl you would have been wretchedly unhappy. I am sure that you would have been kind to the girl and she loved you wholly in return. But, eventually, you would have become indifferent towards her. And when a woman finds out her husband is indifferent towards her, she either becomes dreadful company or begins to seek the company of another woman's husband. Trust me when I tell you the whole thing would have been an absolute failure."

Dorian begrudged her the point. "I suppose you are right. I only thought it was my duty to do so. It isn't my fault that this abhorrent mishap has prevented me from doing what was right. But why can I not feel as deeply about this loss as I want to? I can't be that heartless. Do you think me heartless?"

Lady Helena gave him a melancholy smile as she looked over at the desk. "That foolish love letter is proof that you are not."

His frown deepened. "I am glad you do not think me heartless, for I am nothing of the kind. My heart soars when I hear well-played music and it quickens when I see beauty or appreciate fine craftsmanship. I know am not heartless. And yet, I must admit, I am not as affected by this as I should be. It all seems like the climactic ending to a Greek play that I have taken part in, but have not been truly wounded by."

"Ah, but most seem never to realize when the curtain has fallen. They always wish to continue with another act, rather than to acknowledge that the play has ended. They have no sense of art. Some chose to move on and are consoled by religion. Nothing makes one so vain, as being told they are a sinner. The Conscience makes egotists of us all. Now, there is one consolation which I enjoy more than anything—to take another's admirer when you have lost one of your own. But really, Mr. Gray, Sibyl Vane was so different than most. There was even something quite beautiful about her death. She undoubtedly brought to life the essence of romance, passion, and love."

Dorian's voice dropped to a low murmur. "She will never bring anything to life again."

"No, she will not. But do not forget that unless you have really lived, you have never really died. At least she was to you a tangible dream, filtered through Shakespeare's plays and presented in its loveliest form. But do not mourn for her. Morn for Ophelia, or Cordelia, or the daughter of Brabantio. Do not waste your tears on Sibyl Vane, for she was less real than the characters she portrayed."

A long silence followed. Dorian ran his hand along his face. "Let us not talk again of what has happened. It was simply an incredible experience and that is all. Let us focus on what other unimaginable wonders that life has yet in store for us. I shall join you for the opera this evening. Only let me dress first for the club as we are rather late. Thank you for all that you have said to me. You are undoubtedly my best friend in this world. No one can ever understand me the way that you do."

As Lady Helena left, Dorian again uncovered the screen from the portrait on the wall. Now came the moment to make his choice. Would he choose a life of eternal youth, infinite passion, secret pleasures, wild joys, and elaborate sins? Or had the decision already been made for him? Yes, life had already decided on his behalf. He was to satisfy his unending curiosity of the mysteries that life had to offer. The wolf would, in turn, bear the full burden of his shame. For who would willingly surrender the chance to always remain young and beautiful? Besides, the change was no longer under his control. Why it had happened was really of no importance. What had happened, had happened. He would lock the portrait away and separate it from the sunlight and the condemnations of the rest of the world. A few hours later, he was at the opera with Lady Helena leaning seductively over his chair.

CHAPTER 12.

THE HUNT

Night descended on the wolf's hunting ground. That territory had been growing wider and moving closer to the heart of the city. The forests had recently provided fewer animals to sustain his hunger. Many had been massacred by the wolf and the rest had learned his scent and now gave him a wide berth. Some had abandoned their habitat entirely. The caged prey-animals on the outskirts of the city no longer offered any challenge for the wolf, nor any pleasure in the kill. They were also becoming increasingly better defended by the men that lived in the surrounding villages.

As a result, the wolf had taken to ranging through the stone buildings and paved streets of the town, in pursuit of more challenging prey. He would now take the occasional Bulldog or an unattended carriage horse. Whenever possible, he would stick to the shadows or move amongst the trees of the parks and green areas. Avoiding the detection of man was quite easily done for the cunning beast. If the slightest scent or sound indicated the approach of someone, he could fall onto all fours and lope away at a terrific speed. If needed he would leap high onto buildings and move across the rooftops. His long claws and powerful legs provided all the purchase needed for climbing.

It had been far too long since the wolf had last eaten and the insistent hunger was upon him yet again. The wolf moved through the darkened streets silently. He had the scent of a cart horse and followed along as it moved across the cobbled road. However, he dared not take the animal while the man sat astride the carriage attached to it. After a few more kilometers, he gave up the pursuit to look for more suitable prey. He followed the fading tracks of a pack of stray dogs into an abandoned alley, but was frustrated to find them long gone from the area. It was possible that no sufficient food would be found this night.

The previous night, he had raided the London Zoo. The high iron bars had initially perplexed the wolf. They were stronger and taller than any of the wooden fences he typically encountered. As he circled the zoo, he eventually found a nearby tree that allowed him to jump the spiked fencing. The scents of many new and strange animals excited the wolf as he wandered among the enclosures.

Many of the larger animals seemed too costly to kill, like

the fierce-looking hippo that was over three meters long and weighed nearly three thousand kilograms. Its hide was tough, not to mention it was mostly submerged in a pool of water as it brandished its fearsome tusks. The wolf was also tempted by the large male African elephant. Eventually, he was put off by the almost ten thousand kilogram weight and approximate four-meter height of the thing. The animal also had large tusks and would put up a vicious fight.

He finally settled for taking the striped female zebra that was slumbering in her roofless enclosure. The white and black animal awoke as the bulk of the wolf landed nearby after leaping the fence. She had less than a few seconds to scream and attempt in vain to flee, before the powerful jaws of her attacker ended her once peaceful life. The warm flesh sated his bloodlust. The wolf was able to devour the carcass almost entirely before the night watchman approached on his regular rounds, whistling a tune and swinging his lantern as he walked. The wolf was gone before the watchman knew what was happening.

On this night, the wolf was lurking amongst the tall beech trees in the park of a particularly poor area of town. He abruptly caught a familiar scent—the Master! He was nearby. The wolf ran across the gentle grass in the park and reached the border of the street. Ignoring all caution, the wolf continued to move towards the scent. His movements were brazen in the late hour of the evening and emboldened by the deserted silence of the road.

The wolf was only three meters away from the source of the smell when he stopped and realized his mistake. No, that was not the Master. His scent was there faintly, but it was overlaid onto a mate. The young female. She had recently been cast out from the pack. The stink of shame was upon her. He briefly considered taking her for his own mate, but that would displease the Master. Instead, he retreated behind the bushes and followed her silently, to see what she would do.

Sibyl had been distraught over the breakup for what had seemed like weeks. She could not get over the pain that Dorian had inflicted on her. The bitter tears fell like rain from the sky, leaving dark streaks to mire her otherwise pretty cheeks. A thousand thoughts whirled through her foggy mind. Foremost among them was the confusion and disbelief that her Prince Charming had shunned her. These were followed closely by a terrible emptiness in her heart, and an obsessive replaying of what she had done wrong.

She was so grief struck that it took several moments for her to remember how dangerous it could be to walk home alone in her neighborhood at night. The streets were eerily empty, but she had the nagging feeling that she was being watched. She came to a stop and turned slowly to look behind her. She could see very little from the dimly-lit lamps along the sizable park. She quickened her pace, fear temporarily replacing her wretched sadness. She thought she heard a sound behind her and turned around to look once more. This time, she could just make out two dark-red, glowing eyes. They were watching her amidst the trees and she could see the hazy outline of an enormous, black shape.

The wolf stalked the female silently. He followed her route along the edge of the park. There must be something special about this one for the Master to take such an interest in her. Perhaps it was how small and slender she was, or something about her scent. The wolf drew closer to try and discover the secret. With a start, he realized that the female seemed suddenly aware of his presence. He inhaled the air deeply as the smell of fear unfolded in her.

His blood began to heat at the aroma. The wolf had never before hunted human prey, only animals—for fear of upsetting the Master. But the Master had cast this female out from the pack and now hated her. Even now, the wolf could sense the loathing rolling off her like black waves of mist. She must have greatly offended the Master to make him hate her so. She should be punished. She would be punished. The female turned back, just as the wolf abandoned the cover of trees. She stared unbelievingly at him for a moment, then screamed in a shrill manner and began to run away. The instinct to chase fleeing prey grew too strong to resist. With a growl, the wolf began the hunt.

Sibyl could not believe her blurry eyes. There was a hideous monster in the park and it was staring right at her. She shrieked and her fear spiked as she turned and ran as fast as her slender legs would allow. The terror caused her to move faster than she had in years, since racing with her brother in the open fields as a child. Risking a glance backward, she saw that it was a giant wolf that was rapidly gaining on her. That was impossible, but still she ran. Her house lay on the opposite side of the park, so she turned from the street and took the path of the shortest distance—through the tall trees in the park. Some primal instinct convinced her that if she could just make it to her door, she would be safe.

How different it was to pursue the female than to chase after a simple-minded animal. Wonderfully complex waves of fear wafted off from her as she ran blindly through the trees. The wolf took his time, savoring the pursuit. The female fell over some exposed tree roots and the wolf allowed her the necessary time to regain her feet. The fall had not slowed her down significantly, but she had cut her knee on a jagged rock in the fall. This caused a small amount of blood to flow freely down her leg. Just a whiff of it sent bursts of energy and pleasure through the wolf's body. So, this is what it meant to hunt human prey.

As they reached the middle of the park, the female foolishly tried to hide behind a fallen oak tree. The wolf felt a growing thrill as he let her believe she had evaded him. He circled around the other side. He could hear her breathing as she crouched in the mud. When he was directly behind her, he leaped out to surprise the shaking female. His massive claws swung out at her, but he was surprised as she dodged the blow and dove away from him, rolling in the mud. This was amusing prey. Two more times, the wolf closed on her, each time scoring minor hits from his claws as they raked the female's legs. The bloody lacerations slowed her flight down to a crawl. She screamed and wept as she dragged her injured body across the uneven ground. The wolf waited until she was propped against a large beech tree to make his final advance. He could see the fear in the female's eyes as he rose up onto his hind legs for the killing blow.

Sibyl was in hysterics as she fought against the burning in her legs and the urge to faint away from blood loss. Her breath came in ragged heaves as she struggled to drive oxygen into her lungs. She was barely able to pull herself up against a large beech tree as the beast closed in on her. With horror, she witnessed the animal rise up to its full height on its two hind legs. She realized now that this was not some common wolf, but an abomination out of Hell that was half-man and half-beast.

The creature seemed to take pleasure in her fear and pain. It had a disturbingly intelligent look as it approached her position against the tree. She screamed out for help as the evil animal came within a meter of her. But no one was around to give her aid or to save her from this nightmare. Her Prince Charming had abandoned her and now she was to be murdered by this demon from the Underworld. As the monstrosity's hot, putrid breath hit her face she half-fainted from the severe shock of it all. Relentless pain, fatigue and increasing loss of blood had taken its toll. She was still conscious, but quite dazed. The world took on a dreamlike, fluid quality. When the wolf finally disemboweled her and the vicious jaws closed on her neck, she was lost in the memory of the last time her Prince Charming had removed her dress to make love to her—kissing her neck in that very place.

CHAPTER *13.*

ROMANI SECRETS

Dorian was in the midst of a leisurely breakfast of buttery haddock and ripened fruit when Sage was shown into the room.

She was breathing heavily as though after a brisk walk. "Dorian, thank goodness I have found you. I called on you last night, but they told me you were at the opera. I knew that couldn't be possible and how heartbroken you must be about the whole dreadful thing. But where have you been? Did you go and see the girl's poor mother? She must be besotted with grief. What did she say?"

"My dear Sage, how should I know? I was at the opera with Lady Helena. You should have met us there. Let us not discuss such horrid subjects. If one does not discuss a thing, then it has never happened. Now why don't you tell me about yourself and your latest paintings?"

"You went to the opera?" said Sage, in a slow-strained

voice. "You went to the opera after you heard that Sibyl Vane had been brutally murdered in the street?"

Dorian leapt to his feet and yelled. "Stop, Sage! I will not hear it! What is done is done. What is past is in the past."

"You call yesterday the past?"

"What does it matter how long it has been? A man can master himself and end his sorrow whenever he pleases. I am not at the mercy of my emotions, but rather I control and savor them."

"Dorian, this is horrible! What has changed in you to make you so callous a person? You look like the same wonderful boy who used to sit in my studio, but you are no longer simple, natural, or affectionate. The world has spoiled you and you speak as if you have no heart or pity whatsoever. This must be Lady Helena's influence."

"I owe a great deal to Lady Helena. She has taught me so much about life. You have only taught me about vanity. Now what is it that you want?"

Sage regarded him sadly. "I want back the Dorian Gray that used to sit for me in my studio while I painted, for all those summer afternoons."

"You are so unfair Sage. You come here to console me and then you are furious when you find me consoled. I am no longer that schoolboy. I have developed new passions, new ideas, and a new understanding of beauty. I am much changed, but we are still friends—are we not? I am very fond of Lady

Helena, but you are so much better and stronger. How happy we all used to be together! Please Sage, don't quarrel with me. I am what I am and there is nothing more to say."

The painter felt suddenly moved. She could not reproach dear Dorian any further. After all, he had been a great turning point in her art. "I shan't speak of it again. I trust your name will not be connected to this horrid affair?"

Dorian shook his head. "No, they don't even know my name."

"But surely Sibyl knew your name?"

"Only my Christian name and she never mentioned it to anyone. They were far too curious to learn it and she thought it a fun sport to refer to me only as her Prince Charming. You must make me a drawing of her sometime. I should like to have something more than just broken memories."

"I will draw you something if it pleases you. But you must sit for me again. I simply can't go on without you."

"I can never sit for you again Sage. I am sorry, but it is quite impossible!"

Sage looked at him with shock. "What do you mean? Did you not like the painting of the wolf cub I did for you? Let me see it. Is that what you keep over there behind the screen? It is the finest work I have ever done. Why do you have it covered up in such a way? It is disgraceful to hide my best work like that." Sage scowled and began walking towards the painting.

A cry of terror came from Dorian's mouth and he leaped

between the painter and her artwork. His face took on a ghostly-white pallor. "Sage, you must not look at it. I forbid it."

Sage forced an unbelieving chuckle. "Not view my own work? You can't be serious."

"If you try to look at it Sage, on my honor, I will never speak to you again for as long as I live. I cannot explain and you mustn't ever ask me why. I am very serious about this and if you ever touch that screen, all will be over between us."

Sage was staggered and a look of pain came over her face, as if she had just taken a grievous wound. Her hands clenched and she began to tremble. Dorian had never seen her like this before.

"Dorian. If you don't want me to look at it, I won't. But it all seems rather absurd for me to not view my own work, particularly when I will be exhibiting it in Paris this autumn. It will need another coat of varnish beforehand, so I will have to see it eventually."

Dorian roared in disbelief. "Exhibit it! You want to exhibit it?" An unstoppable feeling of alarm grew in Dorian's chest. Was the whole world to see his terrible secret and know the most intimate details of his life? Impossible. He had to stop it at once.

"Yes of course. You shouldn't object to that. Georges Petit will be showing all my best works in a special collection in the Rue de Seze. It is set to open on the first week of October. The portrait will only be away from you for a month. If you keep it constantly covered by a screen, then you certainly can't care that much for it."

Dorian put his hand to his forehead and felt beads of perspiration gathering there. He was in horrible danger.

He put his face as close to her as it had ever been and fixed her with a serious stare. "Sage, I do have a secret. I will only tell you mine, if you tell me one of yours."

She drew back and quickly looked away. "Dorian, if I told you, you would think less of me and certainly laugh at me. I could not bear either. I will not look at the picture nor share it with the world if it will satisfy you. Your friendship is much dearer to me than any fame or reputation it could bring."

But Dorian was insistent. "No, Sage. You must tell me. I have a right to know the truth." His feeling of terror had been replaced with one of burning curiosity and he was determined to find out what secrets Sage might be hiding. If necessary, those secrets could be used to prevent the portrait from ever being displayed.

Sage's face looked troubled. "Let us sit down, Dorian." They moved to the other side of the room and both sat down in a chair. "Answer me one question. Have you ever noticed anything curious about the portrait?—something that revealed itself to you suddenly?"

Dorian, clutched the arms of his chair with straining fingers. "Sage?"

"I see that you have. Just listen to me for a moment and

hear what I have to say first. As a girl, I grew up in a Romani caravan. I will tell you the tale."

As a young girl, Sage and her family moved constantly from place to place in a Romani caravan. They had a small horse-drawn Vardo with large spoke wheels on the side. It was home to Sage, her mother, and her father. It was cramped but comfortable, with a functioning chimney. It featured a tiny cast-iron stove and a narrow berth that all three shared in the back. Her favorite part though, was the brightly painted wood carvings on the inside walls. Sage's joy in life was painting the intricately carved designs, which her father made on the inside and outside of the Vardo. He was known as a master woodcrafter—when he could get the work. They were not always welcomed by all communities as they traveled. When work was refused to them, they relied on music and fortune telling in exchange for food or money.

Sage was never very good at either, but she loved to draw and paint. When she wasn't helping her mother with the cooking and cleaning, or with foraging for wild berries and nuts, she spent her time drawing. She created detailed animals and intricate faces on any surface available and with any instrument she could find. When her father would return home, the two would work long into the night together to paint the carvings of their home by candlelight.

When she was about ten years old, her father returned from seven days of labor in the nearby fields. She ran to greet him as he set down a coarse sackcloth and said, "Da', yo' home! Can we paint the carvings t'night? Can we please?"

"Arvah, my Chey," he replied, "but dikh, I ha' some drab fo' tu." As he said this, he removed a precious gift that was wrapped carefully in the sackcloth. It was a set of charcoal and oil paints. It had cost nearly all of his wages to buy such an expensive gift.

Tears welled up in Sage's eyes as she hugged her father fiercely. "Thank tu, I'm so baxtalo to have my Da'."

They set to making brushes themselves with hair delicately plucked from the tail of their piebald Cob horse. Sage had raised the horse from a pony and had named him Buttercup. Buttercup was one of her closest playmates and she would spend long hours riding and grooming the horse.

When the paints that her father purchased ran out, her mother took her deep into the forest at night to gather herbs and berries. She taught her the names and uses for all of them. Together they mixed all the different bright colors needed for painting. As the women worked, they would chant in the old tongue. Her mother forbade Sage from doing so when she was not present. One day, she asked her about it cautiously. "Dya, why can't I sing the Romani chants without you?"

"My Chey, it's too dook, ta' mix the drab and the bol. The spells of making are strazhno—too dangerous. Our power comes from the herbs taken from the earth, an' our souls is channeled an' focused thro' our voices. When I tell fortunes, I use the power o' namin', to summon the Mulo spirits. Do no' use these things lightly, an' never link all three."

"I won't Dya." But she practiced all of it as often as she could. If her mother hadn't been so busy with the cooking and cleaning, she would have seen Sage chanting under her breath as she mixed spectacular colors and painted fantastic images.

When she was twelve, Sage began scouring the forest for the perfect color of pink. It could only be found in the rare pyramidal orchid. It was very difficult to find and by the time she had gathered enough for her paints, the sun was hanging low in the sky. In her rush to return home, Sage became hopelessly lost.

Her parents grew worried when their daughter did not return that evening, and set out together with an oil lamp to search the fringes of the dark woods. It was there that they were set upon by a group of local laborers, greatly displeased to have their work taken by the wandering tinkers and who had resorted to highway robbery in the forest. They had been drinking and had worked themselves into a fury over imagined slights and evils at the hands of the Romani people. They seized and beat her parents mercilessly. They spit and cursed at them, before looping two coils of rope around the limbs of a great oak tree. There they hung the husband and wife. The mob exited the forest and found the family's Vardo at the edge of the trees. They burned the beautifully decorated wood to the ground. They mercilessly killed Buttercup and urinated over the corpse.

The next morning, Sage eased the stiffness in her joints caused by a night spent under the stars. She stretched and warmed her hands before making her way towards her home. As she set out, she used the daylight to retrace her steps. She moved quickly, fearful of her parents' anger and worry. The forest was strangely quiet that morning, as if grieving. She reached the clearing where the violence had taken place the previous night. It was the shadows of the two forms swaying lightly in the breeze that she saw on the ground first. She raised her eyes slowly and with a burgeoning sense of dread. At the sight of her dead parents swinging from the trees, her breath was crushed from her chest. She fell to her knees in disbelief and shock. Sobs racked her body as she bawled in dismay and anger. She refused to leave the bodies, but was unable to approach any closer to cut them down.

That was where a kindly old Frenchman named Pascal found her. He had seen the slaughtered horse and burned Vardo along the road at the edge of the forest. He took in the scene and felt a deep pity for the girl, for he was alone in this world as well. He cut down the bodies of Sage's parents and gave them a proper burial in the forest. The girl stood by silently and watched. He covered the filthy and malnourished girl with a blanket and lifted her to the seat of his cart. He took her back to his small home several kilometers away. For days the devastated girl refused to speak. She would eat crusty bread when offered and put on the clothes that Pascal brought her, but her eyes were dull and clouded.

It was only when Sage discovered that Pascal was a painter, that she resumed living. The paint and brushes brought back the spark to her eyes and provided a much-needed distraction. Pascal had no wife or children and was delighted when the girl awakened from her stupor. He cared for the girl as his own and taught her the many painting techniques of the French masters. The two were happy together, or at least found a certain peace amongst their shared passion for artistry. She grew into an accomplished artist and her work and fame soon brought her to the streets of London.

"And that is where I met you, sweet Dorian." Sage sighed, her tale spun. But there was still more that she needed to say.

"From the first moment, you have had the most extraordinary influence on my work. My life has been dominated by you ever since. It was as if you were the realized ideal of every artist's dream. I worshiped you and was immediately jealous of everyone else to whom you spoke. I wanted you all for myself and was only happy when I was with you. Even when you were away from me, you were still with me—in my art. I was too ashamed ever to let you know anything of this. You would not have understood it. I barely understand it myself. I only know that I have seen perfection before my very eyes."

Her eyes wandered around Dorian's face slowly. They paused only as they reached his lips. She continued on tentatively. "Weeks went by and I became more and more obsessed with you. I have drawn you in armor, and as Adonis with spear and cloak. I have painted you on the prow of Adrian's barge as you cross the green Nile and again in some Greek woodland over a still, pool of silver. But that was as art should be—ideal and remote. Do you remember those wonderful summer days we spent together with the wolf cub? How splendid and eternal those afternoons were to me. But then, I decided to paint a portrait of you—as you actually are and in the reality of your own time."

Now that Sage was talking about painting, her voice grew louder and more excited. She gestured with her hands as she continued. "I needed the realism to be exact, so I labored for days to get the perfect skin tones. I agonized over achieving the perfect brush strokes. I called upon all of the skill taught to me by Pascal. I used all of the knowledge passed down to me by my Romani heritage. They were used in gathering and mixing the perfect combination of herbs. This was needed to make my work as lifelike as possible. I may have gone too far when I mixed in some blood from both you and the wolf pup. The mixing of names was another invocation my mother had warned so strongly against. I put too much of myself into the painting. Too much of my idolatry and desire to immortalize you forever—both on the canvas and in my heart."

Sage paused, risking a tentative glance at Dorian to gauge his reaction. He merely sat quietly and stared at her, so she continued speaking. "Later, I felt so foolish and decided that I had imagined everything. I have used similar mixtures and chanted the silly spells of making in my head before. They have never resulted in more than a brighter living-color or a more daring sheen. I was so glad to gift the finished work to you and hardly thought of it again until the offer from Paris came. I see now that you were right Dorian. The picture simply cannot be shown. You must not be angry with me for what I have told you. You are made to be worshipped."

Dorian drew a long breath and a smile came to his lips. The peril was over for now and he was safe again. He felt relief and pity for the girl with her strange confession. Would anyone ever inspire in himself the strange feelings of idolatry that Sage felt?

"Dorian, it is extraordinary that you were able to observe this in the portrait. Perhaps, if not now, maybe someday you would let me stand again in front of the picture."

"Never."

"Well, perhaps that is best and you are right. I owe you so much. Ah! You said you had some secret to tell as well?"

Dorian scoffed. "My dear Sage, what you have told me can hardly be called a secret. You simply admire me too much. That is not even a compliment. It was a very disappointing confession."

"What did you expect? Was there something else about the picture? There is nothing else to see is there?"

"No, nothing else to see. Now, we will no longer speak of it. For we are friends and we must always remain so. You should go and tomorrow I will come to your studio and have tea with you and all will be pleasant again."

Sage gave him a look of relief that the matter was settled. She hated conflict. She slowly rose and moved towards the door. "Very well. Good-bye Dorian. I will see you tomorrow."

After Sage had left, Dorian smirked and chided himself. Poor Sage! She had never even known his true reason for covering the portrait. Instead of revealing his own secret, he had uncovered a very strange secret from his friend. What a bizarre and absurd confession. He sighed and touched the servant's bell that sat on the desk. The portrait would be hidden away at all costs. He could not afford the risk of discovery. He should never have allowed anyone access to the room that it inhabited in the first place.

As he covered the portrait with a heavy coverlet his valet entered. The man stood impassively as he received his orders to frame up the portrait—careful to keep the screen intact, of course.

Briefly, Dorian shuddered and regretted that he had not told Sage the truth about the picture. Since she had created it, perhaps she could have done something to save him. But it was too late now. The future was inevitable. He knew his passions would once more demand to find their terrible outlet. He found solace, knowing that only the painting itself could lay bare the shadow of that evil.

CHAPTER 14.

A WINTER TRYST

When the air began to cool and the days became dreary, Dorian would retreat to his house at Algiers. The journey by boat always cleared his head and the salty sea air did wonders for his constitution. He chartered passage on a three-mast wooden clipper ship called the *Falcon*. The ship had previously been used for the tea trade and was a sleek and speedy vessel. The voyage passed quickly with most of his time spent on deck watching for whales and dolphins. Dorian marveled as the dolphins spun and leapt from the water and the great whales slapped their mighty fins and spouted their defiance high into the air.

The time passed too quickly and soon the ship was docking in the port of Algiers. The French colony offered warm weather and many exotic tastes. His house sat along the beach and offered a stunning view of the bay. He would often be joined by Lady Helena when her husband was called away on business. The two would lay on the warm sand beach and listen as the waves crashed endlessly. They drank marvelous Turkish coffee and sipped sweet mint tea brought by the Arab servants. They spent their days talking about the many wonders of life and made plans to travel the world together.

In the evenings, they would retire with a large bottle of Medea wine and push the limits of physical pleasure. Lady Helena introduced all sorts of riding crops and restraints to the bedroom. She taught him how to intermingle pain with pleasure to achieve a more complicated gratification. They experimented with the hidden arts of the "Kama Sutra", role-played different fantasies, and burned each other with dripped candle wax.

One evening, Lady Helena brought a shy young whore to their bedroom and introduced her as a Tunisian Princess. Her skin was a dark cream color and her brown date-tinted eyes sparkled like the sun reflecting off the water. The thin girl was draped in pink transparent veils that hinted at the curves hidden beneath. She soon put those to use at Lady Helena's command. She began by seductively dancing and gyrating her hips as she clapped together small finger-cymbals. She spun and kicked her long legs while her tight stomach contracted and moved in a way that completely mesmerized Dorian. One by one, the veils were provocatively shed until her small dark nipples were exposed.

Lady Helena observed Dorian's reactions to every

movement with great attentiveness. She smiled as the girl placed a thin veil behind his head and pulled him in close to kiss her perky breasts.

Unable to restrain himself further, Dorian grabbed the girl and roughly threw her onto the bed. Lady Helena held her down as Dorian mounted her and began rutting with little regard for the girl's unintelligible cries of pain. She spoke only Arabic and Dorian merely laughed at the nearly indecipherable babble.

Lady Helena tied the girl's arms firmly to the bedpost with cords of silk and kissed Dorian passionately as he continued to thrust into the helpless girl. As his ardor rose, he placed both hands around the girl's neck and began squeezing. The girl struggled desperately against the restraints in an attempt to draw breath as Dorian continued choking her.

"Call me your Prince Charming," Dorian demanded. The girl did not understand and looked with red-faced fear at her two captors. She could only beg in her native language as Dorian continued. "I said call me Prince Charming!"

He tightened his grip further in anger and ecstasy as he reached climax. With a final shudder, he released his hold and slid off the girl. "What a savage, she couldn't even speak."

Lady Helena's smile faded as she took her eyes off of Dorian for the first time and looked down to the bed. The frail form of the Tunisian Princess was still and motionless. Her eyes stared lifelessly at the ceiling. Lady Helena held her hand to the girl's mouth to check for breath. She looked up slowly at Dorian and spoke in a shocked tone. "You killed her."

"What? That is impossible. I only choked her a little as you and I have done dozens of times."

"You were never so rough before. She is so thin you must have accidentally crushed her. Yes, an accident."

Dorian's face grew panicked. "I couldn't have. Perhaps she was ill. I didn't mean it. You must believe me it was unintentional."

"Something will have to be done about the body. Most of the servants have left for the evening. Go to the garden and find a shovel."

Dorian stared in disbelief at Lady Helena. His gaze slid to the inert form on the bed. Her neck was bruised with purple finger marks. He looked down at his hands in horror. After a moment, Dorian slowly dressed and then went to the garden to find a shovel.

In the pale moonlight, the two began digging a deep hole behind the bushes of the garden. They wrapped the body in expensive bed sheets and unceremoniously dumped it inside. Dorian's taut muscles were straining by the time he had fully covered the hole. Lady Helena calmly transplanted several small saplings in the soil over where the body was buried.

In a cold voice, she whispered, "Let us never speak of this again."

Dorian nodded his assent and the two walked back

wordlessly to the main house. The next day he awoke in the same bed where the girl had died. The bright sun illuminated the room and he looked about for Lady Helena. She was already gone. The servants informed him that she had left to return to London without so much as a farewell note.

Chapter 15.

Human Prey

The wolf had begun hunting human prey. They were plentiful in the dark city streets and provided enough good meat to satiate his gnawing hunger. He was still very careful not to let any who saw him live. To do otherwise would displease the Master. He would only stalk those people that were foolish enough to walk alone in the night.

His favorite victims were the bitches who mated with any males willing to give them the hard coins that they so desired. Their scent during the hunt was intoxicating. He relished the way their faces would twist in fear and the high-pitched screams they made when he finally revealed himself. Their blood tasted sweet as he devoured them. Sometimes he would mate ferociously with them before killing them. Sometimes they did not live through the mating.

The persistent fog of the city hid his movements as he ran between the various parks and green areas. Occasionally as he prowled the night, he would sense a rival of his Master. It was often a rich man that surrounded himself with a large pack and traveled the streets only in the horse carriages. He would spend days following the rival, waiting for a moment when he would finally be alone. This would allow the wolf an opportunity to kill the man who dared to challenge his Master.

These men were not as easy prey as the females. They were usually armed with small "fire sticks" so he had to be sure his approach went undetected. The slightest sound or change in the wind would cause him to abandon his hunt and move away to safety. The wolf hoped the Master would be pleased that he avoided detection and not too angry that he was unable to kill all of his rivals.

Dorian was frequently challenged by other men who were intimidated by his success or popularity. His greatest adversary was Sir Robert Medcalf. The two had become enemies over some imagined slight Dorian had supposedly caused to his unwed sister. The girl had been pretty but hardly special in any way. He had only bedded her a few times but her fiancé had caught wind of it and ended the engagement publicly. Now the girl was disgraced and no other suitable matches could be found.

Sir Robert had become enraged and now made it his mission in life to thwart Dorian in every way possible. He was quite an influential man and unfortunately had the ear of the Duke of Berwick. He used his many connections to try to poison many in society against Dorian by making titles and permits much more difficult to obtain, and the man had even sunk so low as to engage in vexatious litigation in the courts. Dorian was forced to spend a great deal of time and money defending himself against the unfounded allegations. He hated him with a deep passion. Dorian had finally had enough when Sir Robert tried to have him blackballed at yet another club. He vowed to end the man and began formulating a careful plan.

Dorian began to establish trust with his enemy through a series of cryptic letters sent under an assumed name. According to these letters, Dorian was a likeminded gentleman whose sister had also fallen prey the charismatic Dorian Gray. He claimed to desire an alliance with Sir Robert. He suggested that the two pool their resources against their shared enemy and finally bring about a deciding victory against him. Dorian had even gone so far as to provide financial backing for several of Sir Robert's latest endeavors against him. That final gesture had finally convinced Sir Robert to agree to a secretive meeting in an abandoned building near the factory district of Birmingham.

When Sir Robert arrived at the prescribed hour, he found the dilapidated building deserted. There was a letter sitting on a lone barrel of oil in the center of the room. Sir Robert cut open the letter and read it aloud.

My Dear Sir Robert Medcalf,

I am afraid that the allegations against Mr. Dorian Gray regarding your sister are quite true.

Please excuse my inability to meet with you this evening. I am currently occupied in buttering her bun and Mr. Gray and myself are taking turns rogering her at this very moment.

I assure you that trollop's cock alley has become quite well worn.

Your loyal co-conspirator
Mr. Dorian Gray

Sir Robert began cursing and ripped the letter to shreds. He looked up sharply as the only door to the room slammed shut. He ran over just in time to hear a heavy beam fall into place, barring the door.

"Now look here Dorian, this ruse has gone on long enough. I assure you the Duke of Berwick will hear of this outrage. Unbar the door at once!"

However, the only response was the sound of laughter as Dorian kicked over another barrel of oil and dropped a lit torch to the floor. Sir Robert's threats quickly turned into screams as the building was consumed by fire.

CHAPTER 16.

THE DUEL

On one occasion in the early springtime, Dorian was riding through the country near Trouville with his young friend Lord Crawley. Lord Crawley was very tall, with dark features including short black hair and a thin mustache. He was dressed splendidly in a silk hunting shirt and tight, leather riding trousers. He was riding a fierce-looking, white Kochlaini Arabian horse. To Dorian he was a like-minded gentleman, with a large fortune and obscure desires—quickly resulting in the two becoming fast friends.

Dorian was riding a haughty, charcoal-black Godolphin Barb horse and was dressed in a similar fashion. His look however, was a stark contrast with a clean-shaven face. His longer, unruly blonde hair moved freely in the wind as the two rode together. They were discussing Lord Crawley's favorite topic—female conquests and the details surrounding them.

Lord Crawley expertly raised his leather reins and

slightly bent his knees in the stirrups as he prepared for the jump over a large oak tree that had fallen to the ground. "She was insatiable, you see. She couldn't get enough of me. I was exhausted from taking her to my bed two, three times a day—or would have if not for my daily exercise regime, of course." He paused as they approached the obstacle.

The pair increased their mounts' pace to a canter and leaned forward. They lifted their bodies off the leather of the forward seat saddles. The two thoroughbreds easily cleared the downed tree with leaps that landed cleanly and left plenty of room to spare.

"Well, it's not in the quantity but in the quality, my good man."

"Ha! You are one to speak of quantity. I have seen the procession of young ladies that grace your bedchamber. But this church bell had quality all right! A right bushel bubby that one was. She is a classic red-head with tiny pink nipples set atop gloriously perky breasts. They saluted whenever I entered the room. She has a tiny waist and long, slender legs. And what a nancy that one had." He smacked the behind of his horse with his riding crop to underscore the final point.

"At any rate, I do hope you were able to prolong your time in the commodity this time by using the techniques we discussed."

"Oh, yes. We would knock for hours. One time I gave the girl a green gown on the lawn of her father's estate."

"Smashing! But have you had occasion to—," Dorian cut off as they came upon two gentleman along the roadway who were also mounted. They were well-equipped, though on lesser brown-Cob horseflesh.

Dorian was quite startled to see that the riders were none other than Lord Donohoe and his lesser-known brother. Lord Donohoe was dressed plainly in simple brown riding trousers and a matching coat. His greying hair was cut smartly in the military style. A door-knocker beard and mustache adorned his face. His brother attired himself in a comparable manner. All four of the horses slowed to a walk as they approached, with Dorian reigning up when they were a few meters away.

Dorian called out a greeting. "Good afternoon Lord Donohoe. I was unaware that you had a residence in Trouville."

"There are many things you mistakenly think me unaware of—you cussed bedswerver!" With that insult, Lord Donohoe removed his riding glove and threw it to the ground before bellowing his challenge to Dorian. "I demand satisfaction for what you have done to my daughter!"

Dorian's reply was smooth and in blatant disregard for the challenge to duel that was just laid before him. "My dear man, I believe there has been some case of mistaken identity. I do not even know your daughter."

"Liar! Scoundrel! I know what you have done to her, corrupting her mind and body. It is by your hand that she has become nothing more than a common dollymop."

"Take care with your insults sir. I assure you, I have nothing to do with your daughter's poor choices in life. I will not tolerate your slander any further."

"Then you will face me today on the field of honor and pistols will decide the truth of it!"

Dorian saw that Lord Donohoe was resolute in his challenge. He took stock of the older man's frail stature, and the slight shaking of his pointing hand.

He sighed and lifted his hands in a gesture of compliance. "Very well. If you insist on this course we will play it out. But let it be known that I attempted to move you from it." With that, Dorian swiftly dismounted in a fluid motion and beckoned to his friend. "Lord Crawley will act as my second, as I am sure your brother will act as yours. Since you have determined the choice of weapons and the time of the duel, I will determine the ground and the form to be followed."

Dorian gestured towards a small clearing behind the group. "We will meet in the small field behind you and begin back-to-back. Following ten paces on my count, we will both turn and shoot. Are these terms acceptable to you sir?"

Lord Donohoe and his brother dismounted in response. They moved briskly to the prescribed field and the seconds began to inspect the pistols that Lord Donohoe produced from a cherry wood case, carried on his saddlebag. The selected weapons were brown-barrel, octagonal sighted, Percussion 14 bore pistols. They could be loaded with only one lead ball at a time.

Lord Crawley picked up the weapons and checked the firing mechanism on each one. "They are balanced and level, Dorian. They appear adequate and should produce a straight shot."

Dorian liked his chances in this contest, for he was no stranger to firearms and was an accomplished marksman. He regularly hit his target when shooting at cans or stuffed animals on the firing range and he had brought down many a stag and quail while hunting. His opponent was nearly two decades his senior and of questionable health. However, he had never before killed a man with a firearm. At that moment, Lord Donohoe began a coughing fit as he was preparing himself. Dorian smiled and offered his handkerchief, which was harshly refused. He confidently selected his weapon and assumed his position. There was always a chance that both combatants would miss. Then the matter would be concluded without bloodshed. When Lord Donohoe finally regained his breath, he approached with the second pistol in his hand and the two stood back-to-back.

"This is your last chance to withdraw your challenge," whispered Dorian.

"And your last chance to pray to God for forgiveness," Lord Donohoe responded curtly.

Dorian cocked his weapon and heard the sharp click as

his opponent did the same. The gun felt strangely heavy in his hand. The grip seemed suddenly slick, as sweat began to form in his palm and along the top of his hand. Now was the moment for steely resolve.

In a scratchy voice he shouted out, "Begin!" and started counting off the ten paces in a measured tone. He was surprised at the trepidation he felt and the thundering of his heart beating in his ears. True, he had never fought in a duel before but surely it was not a difficult thing. He was young and strong and would certainly triumph. It was only a matter of breathing and aiming carefully. There was no chance of this old man besting him.

The wide field where they dueled was really a picturesque sight. It was framed by a small blue stream with two large weeping willows on either bank. They each dropped spiral-green strands into the gently flowing water. Stubborn wildflowers grew everywhere in whites, blues, and oranges. On the other side of a light-colored beech fence a herd of creamy-white cattle grazed, indifferent to the drama unfolding so close by. The sky was clear and filled with the bright-warmth of a bold, yellow sun. It seemed as if you could see for kilometers in every direction. What a beautiful place this would be to meet one's end.

The count reached ten and Dorian began turning. As he spun he started to level his pistol as he raised his arm. He was startled to see that his aged opponent had already completed his turn by pivoting smartly on his heel. He was expeditiously aiming his pistol in Dorian's direction, unmistakably preparing to fire. Dorian struggled to make up the lost time—too late. Lord Donohoe fired his pistol with a crack like thunder, sending up an acrid cloud of black smoke. The 44 caliber lead ball exploded through Dorian's shoulder. The soft lead flattened and expanded as it exited out his back, leaving a wound the size of a pomegranate. The pain was excruciating and Dorian cried out. As his knees buckled, he gritted his teeth and fired blindly into the smoke in front of him before passing out.

Dorian awoke in the plush, canopied bed of his villa. His dreams had been filled with blood and death. He remembered running through a misty field at night, tripping over the dismembered bodies of friends and loved ones. Their faces were pale and bloated. No matter how quickly he ran, the field seemed to never end. Just a dream. Perhaps the duel had been a dream as well. Then his hand found the side of his riding trousers. He looked down in surprise. His clothing was the same that he had been wearing on the field and was now covered in dirt and blood. Exhaustion lay heavy on his body, as if he was drowning at the bottom of the sea in a full suit of armor.

Lord Crawley was suddenly there at his side with a worried look on his face. "Dorian, are you feeling well? You are very fortunate that Lord Donohoe's aim was off. Apparently, he was once renowned for his dueling prowess as a Captain in the Army."

Dorian's confusion reached his voice. "You mean, he missed? I was certain that I was hit. Are you quite sure? What of Lord Donohoe?"

"Well he must have missed for here you are, whole and sound. Your aim however, was true. It was really a fantastic shot. I've never quite seen the like. Your ball took him right between those beady little eyes of his and he was killed instantly. His brother was very distraught and has taken the body away. Dorian, you've won!"

Dorian looked around tentatively at his surroundings. "I've won? But, how did I get here?"

"When I saw you were unconscious I rode back for help. I thought for sure you had been injured. Your valet and I brought a wagon and together we lifted you from the field and transported you here. You were breathing quite rapidly, so we put you straight into bed while the valet went for the doctor. I am sure that won't be needed now, your color seems quite restored."

"Yes, I am fine. Please, there is no need for a doctor."

"Very well, but are you sure you weren't grazed in the arm by the shot? There was quite a lot of blood but we were amiss as to its origin. The whole matter is inextricable."

Dorian was silent and fingered the spot on his chest where the ball had entered his skin. The clothing was ripped and torn, exposing the flesh beneath. There was no wound there, not even a scratch. But his finger could feel dried blood. Had it been his imagination? Then whose blood was it?

Dorian placed his hand on his chin speculatively. "Perhaps Lord Donohoe's aim was so bad, his ball struck a passing bird from the sky. Yes that must be it."

Lord Crawley laughed. "Capital! Quite right. When the doctor arrives, I will let him know his service is no longer needed and see he receives compensation for his trouble. Now, get some rest and when you are recovered we will invite the Eldritch sisters to dine with us."+

Lord Crawley excused himself from the room and exited quietly. Dorian wearily rose from his mahogany bed and decided he should change into a fresh shirt and trousers. He moved to the washbasin and stripped off his clothes. After filling it with water, he carefully cleaned away the dried blood on his chest. He turned around slowly in the mirror, only to discover a larger mass of red caked on his back. This too he cleaned, while contemplating what it all might mean. How had he healed so quickly and perfectly from the wound? It was Impossible.

The duel made Dorian even more paranoid that someone might discover his many secrets. He cut short his holiday in the country and returned home. After a time, he could no longer endure to be long away from England. He gave up the villa, as well as the house at Algiers where he and Lady

Helena had spent so many pleasant winters together. He couldn't abide to be separated from the picture that was now so much a part of his life. There was always the nagging fear that someone might gain access to the room, despite the elaborate bars that covered the door. Sometimes, while entertaining at his great house in Nottinghamshire, he would inexplicably take leave of his guests to rush back to town. He could not be at peace until he examined the door and made certain the picture was still held safely within. What if it was stolen from him? Then the world would know his secret. Perhaps they already suspected.

CHAPTER 17.

WHISPERED CONVERSATIONS

Several days later, Dorian took his Hyson green tea in the drawing room and began reading the evening paper. He was shocked at what he saw on the fifth page of *The St. James*:

INQUEST ON AN ACTRESS.—An inquest was held this morning at the Bell Tavern, Hoxton Road, by Mr. Marlow, the District Coroner, on the body of Sibyl Vane, a young actress recently engaged at the Royal Theatre, Holborn. An open verdict was returned as the cause of death is still being investigated. Considerable sympathy was expressed for the mother of the deceased, who was greatly affected during the giving of her own evidence, and that of Dr. Ashford, who made the post-mortem examination of the deceased.

The paper was filled with an unusually large number of inquests resulting in verdicts of murder, manslaughter, or with undetermined cause of death. It appeared that Jack the Ripper and the High Rip Gang were growing increasingly out-of-hand and the authorities were powerless against them. Several pages also decried the recent rise in attacks on farm animals in the surrounding areas. The suspected culprit was a feral pack of Bulldogs which were running wild and terrorizing the countryside.

He grimaced, tore the paper in two, and flung the pieces away. How horrid the whole matter was. But at least no one suspected his involvement. What had Dorian Gray to do with her death? He had not been the one that had killed her.

As was to be expected, the inquest came to nothing. Everyone moved forward with their lives as did the ever-changing seasons. Dorian glorified in the experiences of life and the many pleasures that it had to offer him. Whenever a strange rumor about his conduct surfaced in the chatter of London clubs, it was quickly dismissed and explained away by those who saw his perfect, unblemished face.

Those who spoke evil against Dorian Gray fell silent whenever he entered the room. The unassailable purity of his visage provided the strongest rebuke that could be made. His very demeanor recalled a memory of innocence and replaced the tarnished one which flew behind closed doors like a specter of whispered conversations. It caused bewilderment that one so charming and graceful could so elegantly escape the stain of age. He was immune to the growing dread that others felt amongst all the violence and uncertainty.

Those who thought themselves his friends increasingly noticed Dorian's disappearances, leaving them to ruminate on the cause of such mysterious and prolonged absences. The nature of these forays gave rise to much conjecture by all in society. Upon returning, Dorian would creep upstairs to the locked room. He could often be seen wearing a key on a fashioned silver chain around his neck. These days it never left his sight. He would stand in front of the portrait that Sage had painted and stare at it for hours. He grew more enamored of his own beauty and more intrigued in the corruption of his own soul.

Many a sleepless night passed in his delicately scented bedchamber, or in some fetid, sordid room of a tavern by the docks. He would think on the ruin that he had brought upon his soul and the curiosity of life—which increased with each gratification he indulged in. The more knowledge he possessed, the more he desired. He had taken to using assumed names and disguises when he frequented various dens of iniquity so that his secrets could stay just that. But his mad hungers continued to grow more ravenous the more that they were fed.

He would try to strike a sort of balance. Once or twice a week, Dorian would open his elegant home to the world and throw lavish parties. He invited the most celebrated musicians and renowned artists. Lady Helena was always quick to assist in any preparations that were needed. An invitation to such an event was most coveted. This was particularly the case among the very young women who viewed Dorian Gray as the ultimate realization of scholarly culture and distinction. To them he was a true citizen of the world.

His fancy dictated all the hottest trends in the arts and fashion. His uncommon mode of dress and unique style could be marked on all the young exquisites of the Mayfair balls. They copied him in club windows in every way—yet they always fell half-short when trying to reproduce his accidental charm and unintentional grace.

He began to gather to himself all things of beauty and rarity. This included alluring jewels, delicate silks, sophisticated perfumes, rare works of art, exquisite furniture, renowned musical instruments, ancient manuscripts, archaic scrolls, imported pieces from faraway lands, coveted textile and embroidered works, rich tapestries, faded frescoes, and all types of lattice and vermilion and gold. These he pursued with gusto and lost himself in the pursuit.

He would have some measure of joy for a short time, as he examined a new item that he had come to possess. But always Dorian would grow saddened by thinking of the ruin that time would bring to these beautiful and wondrous things. Somehow he had managed to escape the effects of time. They would fade and turn to dust while he remained the same. Summer followed summer, the nights of horror and degradation repeated—but he was always unchanged.

After Dorian passed his thirty-fifth year, curious accounts of his activities began to emerge. These placed him in company with shifty sailors, wanted thieves, and deceitful coiners in the low dens of Whitechapel. He was nearly blackballed at the West End club. On one occasion, while entering the smoking-room of the Churchill, the Duke of Berwick got up in a most marked manner and went out very abruptly. Dorian's absences from society became notorious. Men would mutter to each other in corners or pass him with a sneer of contempt set upon their face. Others would look at him with cold, searching eyes as if in an attempt to uncover his secrets.

Of course, Dorian took no notice of such slights and the petty insolence of others. His frank manner, boyish smile, and infinite youth were sufficient answer to any whispers that circulated around him. However, it was remarked that some of those with whom Dorian had seemed most intimate appeared after a time to shun him completely. Women who had once wildly adored him and had thrown caution and social convention to the wind for his sake, were now seen to grow pale with horror or red with shame whenever Dorian Gray entered the room.

Despite that, these minor scandals only increased his flourishing fame. Along with his apparently vast wealth, it only served to cement him as a requisite element of society. A Civilized society can never really believe anything too detrimental of the rich and fascinating. For they understand that good manners are vastly more important than good morals. They are far more likely never to forgive a man who throws a boring party, serves cheap wine, or prepares a tasteless dinner. Too many were enamored with Dorian Gray's opinions on life. He often expressed that life was really a mixture of multiple lives. It was a myriad of sensations, strange legacies of thought and passions, and with everything including the very flesh—tainted by the lives of the dead who came before us.

CHAPTER *18.*

THE FOG

On the ninth of November, Dorian was walking home near eleven o'clock at night after dining with Lady Helena. He was wrapped in heavy furs against the frigid and foggy night. The street was veiled in a weighty mist, the streetlights glowing in blanketed orbs of grey. They cast strange silhouettes on the swirling vapor that hovered above the ground. As he moved along, unable to see but a few feet ahead, he had the strange sensation that he was being followed. There was a familiarity to the presence that he couldn't quite place. A sense of instinctual fear came over him, which he quickly dismissed. Any miscreant would also be swallowed in the enveloping white shroud and would find his path difficult, if not impossible, to track.

At the corner of Grosvenor Square and South Audley Street, a woman passed him in the haze. She was wearing a mink coat and walking very quickly by with a heavy cowhide bag in her hand. Though blurry in the fog, he recognized the gait and dress of the woman. It could belong to none other than his estranged friend, Sage. Dorian made no sign of recognition but went hurriedly on in the direction of his own house, hoping he had not also been recognized in the gloom. But she had seen him. Her footsteps stopped on the pavement about a meter after they passed each other and then the sound turned and began hurrying after him. In a few moments her hand was on his arm.

"Dorian! What an extraordinary piece of luck! I have been waiting for you in your library since nine o'clock. Finally I took pity on your valet and sent him home. He was anxious to begin his holiday this weekend. I am off to Paris myself, by the midnight train then ferry. I needed to see you before I left. Strange, I thought I had seen two shapes dressed in heavy fur coats as you passed me, but now I see that it was just you. Didn't you recognize me?"

"Not in this murk, Sage. Why, I can barely see my own hand right in front of my own face. I am sorry to hear that you are going away, I have not seen you for ages. I suppose you will be returning soon?"

"No, I will be away from England for at least six months. I will be working in a small studio in Paris on a new great work that I have trapped in my head. But let us go inside and talk for a moment."

"I would be quite pleased to do so. But won't you miss

your train?"

"I have at least an hour and I have already sent on ahead the majority of my luggage. All that I have with me is my bag."

"What an adventure. Come let us get out of this frigid fog and into the warmth of the house."

With that the two made their way quickly down the empty street and up the steps to Dorian's door. They went inside and were greeted by the light of a pleasant fire and the lamps still lit. The two hung up their coats and Sage placed her bag in the corner. After they were seated, Dorian served the brandy-and-soda himself—now regretting allowing his valet to leave early on holiday. Sage spoke up immediately. "Now, Dorian I want to speak to you quite seriously."

He answered her in a petulant voice. "Whatever is the matter?"

"Dorian, you need to know that people are saying the most dreadful things against you in London. They are talking as if you are some vile and degraded fiend. Mind you, I don't believe these rumors at all. When I look at your face, I can't believe them. Sin is something that cannot be hidden. It is written plain across one's countenance. Whereas your face is so pure and innocent from any fault. I see you so seldom now, you never come by the studio anymore to visit. But tell me Dorian, why a man such as the Duke of Berwick leaves a room when you enter? How is it that so many other gentlemen refuse your invitations to dine at your house, and never invite you to dine at theirs?"

Sage paused with tears brimming her eyes. Dorian extended his handkerchief to her and she dabbed her eyes before continuing. "Do you remember Lord Crawley? The two of you were once such close friends. I met him at dinner last week. When your name came up in the conversation he curled his lip and remarked that no pure-minded girl should ever be introduced to you, nor any chaste woman even sit in the same room as you. I told him I was a friend of yours and asked him his meaning. He gave me so many terrible examples! He mentioned the wretched Pickering girl who committed suicide, and Sir Robert Medcalf who left England with a ruined name. He spoke of the dreadful end that befell Clara Cosgrove. What about the young Duchess of Perth? What sort of life will she have now and who will associate with her? What of Lord Donohoe, who was so broken with shame and sorrow over the fate of his only daughter—only to disappear entirely."

Dorian's voice was heavy with contempt as he answered. "Stop it Sage! You have no idea what you are talking about. How could Berwick *not* leave a room when I enter, when I know everything of his life, and he knows nothing of mine? Did I force the Pickering girl to end her own life? Did I teach Sir Robert Medcalf his vices? Did I force Clara Cosgrove into a life of debauchery? If the Duchess of Perth has taken to writing her friend's names across her bills, how am I her keeper? What is it to me if Lord Donohoe's daughter has taken to the streets and he has fled the country in disgrace? It is all the mindless chatter of the middle classes and their moral prejudices. They simply pretend to be part of intelligent society, while they ignore their own sins and slander their betters."

Sage was no longer able to stop the tears from tumbling down her cheek. "Dorian that is not what I am asking you. I know that England is a corrupt and evil place. The people here have developed a delirium for pleasure. But they have sunken even further down into the depths and all claim that it is you who have led them there."

"You go too far."

"I must speak, and you must listen. When you first met Lady Collingwood, she was untouched by any thread of scandal. Now, no decent woman will drive with her in the park. Even her children are forbidden from living with her. There are all these terrible tales of you seen creeping about at dawn, leaving from dreadful houses and slinking about in disguise. Your face has been associated with all of the foulest dens in London. Are these rumors true? Can they be? I don't mean to preach at you, but you should live a life that commands the respect that you deserve. I want you to clear your name and end your association with these dreadful people. Let your influence be used for good and not evil."

Sage paused and looked at Dorian with an imploring look, wanting to see the good in him.

"Go on Sage, finish what you have to say to me."

"You must give me some answer to these horrible charges against you. Tell me they are false and I will believe you. Deny them! I wonder, do I even know the real Dorian Gray? I should like to see your soul."

"See my soul!" Dorian exclaimed as he leapt up from the sofa, his complexion turning white with fear.

"Yes," answered Sage, "but only God can do that."

A laugh of mockery broke from his lips. "But you shall see it for yourself, you shall be as God—tonight! Come, the inconceivable truth is written in your very own handiwork. You might as well look at it now. Witness the corruption of it face-to-face."

With a mad sort of pride, Dorian picked up a small lamp and beckoned Sage to follow him. He started up the stairs towards the locked room above. As they reached the top of the landing, Dorian set down the lamp and opened the metal bars with his well-worn key. He hesitated for a moment and turned to Sage.

"You are the only person in the world who is entitled to learn this secret about me. You have more to do with forming my life than you know."

They entered together and Dorian shut the door behind them and locked it. Sage glanced around with a puzzled expression. The room had not been lived in for many years. It was bedraggled and empty, save for a lone open armchair and ebony lamp table. Most of the room was covered with a film of dust and an alarmed mouse ran silently through a ragged hole that was chewed into the corner wall.

Dorian gestured to the stained shroud hanging on the wall. "Is it only God that can see the soul, Sage? Draw back that filthy curtain and see mine."

"You are mad Dorian."

"So you won't do it? Then I must reveal it myself." With that Dorian tore the curtain from the metal rod and flung it savagely to the ground.

A gasp of horror escaped from her lips as she saw the hideous beast that was depicted on the canvas. The once-innocent wolf cub had grown immense and was now the most gruesome thing that she had ever seen. It had changed into a terrifying beast, whose shape now dominated almost all of the picture—save the beautiful, smiling face of Dorian in the background. Its elongated fangs and treacherous claws were covered in a black foulness that could only be rotten, hardened blood. The sinew and muscles had grown more pronounced, but also more sickly. It looked wrong in a way that compelled the eye to shy away from the raw savagery of it. And the face—that was the most frightful thing of all. The eyes of the monstrosity glowed blood-red with hate. They bore down into the very depths of the soul, seeking to devour any light or goodness found there. They spoke of a deep and unquenchable thirst for blood and violence. They were calculating, cruel, and disturbingly intelligent—as only a man's eyes could be.

Tears came unbidden to Sage's eyes. It was impossible. Who had done this wretched thing? To paint over the small wolf cub with such vile menace. Yet, she seemed to recognize her own brushwork. The creation was too terrible to comprehend and she became afraid. She seized a lighted candle and held it up to the picture. Surely it was some foul parody. A joke of some sort. That was not her picture. But it was. Her thoughts went back to the wolf that had bitten her hand before returning to the forests. It had not been seen since.

All the reports of animals being killed savagely in the surrounding areas now seemed to make sense. But what about the killings of people, the murders of innocent citizens? Was it not the handiwork of Jack the Ripper, marauding gangs, or vicious Bulldogs? She felt an icy surety now that the responsible party was this beast depicted on the canvas in front of her. Her artist's eyes detected a resemblance to the wolf that she had so lovingly raised. It could be seen there in the color of the mane and here in the angle of the maw. Was this what had become of the wolf that had deserted and betrayed her?

Dorian merely stood there, leaning against the black-marble fireplace mantel and observing Sage's reaction.

Sage begged for answers in a quiet voice. "What does this mean? It is impossible. I don't believe that this is my picture."

"You don't see your handiwork in it?"

"There was nothing evil or shameful in what I painted. I knew I shouldn't have put so much of myself into the work. I shouldn't have mixed bloods and herbs into the paints. I shouldn't have spoken the old words and the spell of making. Most of all, I shouldn't have linked your names together. I should have listened to my mother's warning. But how could the wolf have been corrupted so?"

"It is the face of my soul."

"It is a demon!"

Dorian replied with a shrug of despair. "Everyone has both heaven and hell in them Sage."

Sage turned back to the portrait. "If this is what you have done with your life then you must be even worse than they say."

Her hand shook, and the candle fell to the floor and began sputtering. She flung herself to the chair by the window and buried her face in her hands to weep. Soon, both she and Dorian were sobbing quietly.

The tears flowed freely from her eyes. "Dorian, we must pray. We must pray for forgiveness and to have our sins washed away. Come, let us pray together."

"It is too late for that."

"It is never too late, Dorian. Come kneel down with me now. Can't you see the way in which that accursed thing leers at us?"

Sage fell to her knees with a pleading look.

Dorian looked once more at the picture. Suddenly, an uncontrollable feeling of hatred for Sage came over him. Rage and violence warred within him. He loathed this woman kneeling on the floor by the window. It was her doing that had caused this. Her fault. She had to be stopped—killed!

An explosion of sharp glass and bent metal flung Dorian back from the window. An enormous dark shape crashed through the pane and struck the kneeling form of Sage. As Dorian slammed to the ground his ears were filled with the sound of a terrible growl. It rose above the crashing, tearing, and wet smacking noises. Dorian turned his head to see Sage set upon by the beast from the picture. A stifled scream and the sound of choking on blood came from Sage's mouth. The brute rose and descended again and again on her form. She was child-sized next to the huge, hairy figure. The claws continued to render flesh and began disemboweling her. With blood splattering everywhere, Sage had only a moment to begin shrieking in pain before the heavy jaws descended upon her throat. They ripped out the delicate flesh there—cutting off all sound. In her last few seconds of life, Sage locked eyes with Dorian in an accusatory stare. Her arms and legs convulsed with a mind of their own, her blood flowing freely onto the floor as she died.

For a few moments his hearing and vision left him and an enveloping darkness seemed to descend around him. A moment later, his hearing returned first. It was filled with a ragged breathing. The panting was wet with blood and slowing, as from an athlete completing a long run. He heard the great figure shift and turn—long claws scouring the floor as they moved.

As his vision restored, he could make out the giant form. The beast had turned from Sage and now looked at him with those glowing, red eyes. Dorian was sure that at last his life was over. But the beast only remained still. Motionless. Waiting. Carefully, Dorian rose to his side. There was no response from the monster except for the movement of the huge nostrils, which expanded and contracted as if taking in his scent. Several more moments passed without any other motion from the pair.

Dorian rose tentatively to his feet, leaning heavily upon the table. Amazingly, the creature seemed to back away and lower its head, breaking eye contact. That's right. Now he remembered. Dorian was the pack leader to this wolf. He reached out with his senses and felt the renewed connection that he and the wolf had once shared when it was still a normal wolf and not this—thing. He was abruptly confident that the animal would do him no harm. Dorian began to pace the room.

Dorian did his best to fill his voice with a scolding tone as he continued to observe the creature's reaction. "What have you done you vile beast? We will be discovered for sure." The creature knew that it was being rebuked and lowered his ghastly head further, eyes downcast towards the floor.

But was that true? Would they be discovered? Certainly, there had been a rather loud crash and other—noises. But how effective was the deep, London fog at distorting and concealing sounds? He went over to the landing and listened to the street outside. Everything was absolutely quiet. The hour was late and no one was about. There was hardly any light to be seen on the vacant street. The constables must be currently far away on their rounds of the silent houses, shrouded in white fog.

Everything was still in the house. The valet! No—he had left on holiday earlier that evening. He turned back to the hulking wolf. He could see that it waited on his command. Quickly, Dorian's mind formulated a plan.

"Can you understand me?"

The ears perked up and turned forward. The murderous eyes raised and softened, as the terrifying head tilted ever so slightly at an angle—as if to listen.

"I can see that you do. Very well, take Sa—the body, as far away from here as you can. Do not be seen. I suppose you are most adept at that. Make sure the body is never discovered. Devour it if you must, but do so fully. Sage left on the midnight train and nothing must link her remains to me or my home. Now, go!"

The immense claws seized onto the bloody mass of meat with disturbingly strong hands. The canines of the great beast sank into the flesh with a surprising delicateness. It lifted its kill from the bloody floor and moved towards the shattered window. With a final piercing look, the towering creature leapt away using its powerful hindquarters. It sailed through the broken window and crashed into the soft garden below.

Dorian collapsed to the floor in relief. He strained his brain as he thought quickly. Sage had left the house at eleven and dismissed the valet. No one had seen him come in again. As far as anyone knew, Sage was on her way to Paris. She would be gone for six months or a year before suspicions would be roused. All of the evidence could be cleaned up and destroyed long before then.

The servants were surprised to find their master hard at work as they arrived. He was shoveling fresh mulch and moving debris in the garden in a most vigorous manner. It was not unusual for their master to quickly change his fancies and this week it was apparently gardening. They were quite used to his eccentrics by now and could only smile and agree as he began giving orders.

"Ah, quickly now! Help me move away that brush from the old rose bushes. I've decided the garden is quite overdue for a renovation, you see. And naturally, this must include removing that small, old window that overlooks the garden. It will be replaced with a new large-pane, machine-polished glass. They are quite fashionable. I'm afraid I got quite carried away in starting the demolition myself and have done just a horrid job. Send for someone from the James Powell & Sons glassworks at once to finish the job."

Dorian made a point to speak to his valet in front of the other servants. "I came home so late on the evening before you began your holiday. Tell me, did anyone call?"

"Lady Holdsworth the artist, sir. She stayed until eleven, then went off to catch her train."

"Oh! I am sorry I didn't see her. Did she leave any message?"

"No, sir. Except that she would write to you from Paris."

"That will do, thank you."

CHAPTER 19.

THE DOCKS

An icy rain fell as Dorian rode in a second-rate hansom that moved briskly along the banks of the swelling River Thames. He was dressed commonly with the rough clothes of a laborer and a muffler wrapped about his throat. He wore a shabby bowler hat, pulled down to cover his forehead. The street lamps blurred in the dripping mist, as downtrodden men and demoralized women left the now closing public-houses along the route. As the streets drew closer together, all sorts of ruffians could be seen. They clustered together in groups, forming wicked plans to enrich their fortunes. In one crumbling bar with the sign of a rearing stallion out front, drunkards brawled and a straggled scream shattered the quiet of the night.

The engorged moon hung full and low in the sky like a yellow skull. Misshapen clouds stretched across the floating orb with elongated hands and bony fingers grasping. As they neared the docks, the gas lamps grew fewer and the streets gloomier. The cobblestones blackened as they passed the deserted brickfields. Bottle-shaped kilns spat their outrage with orange tongues of fire into the cooling air. Mangy dogs snarled in hunger and wandering sea-gulls screamed their displeasure at the hansom's passage.

The windows lining the rough-paved streets were mostly dark now. The driver turned down a dim lane with low roofs and jagged chimney-stacks. The black masts of the ships could be seen as a backdrop to the rooftops. Wreaths of white mist clung like ghosts to their yards.

Dorian called out to the driver in an altered voice. "This will do." The driver answered by slowly bringing the hansom to a halt. He exited and paid the man hastily with a handful of coins before turning to walk briskly towards the quay. As he walked down the empty street he was sure to glance back occasionally, careful to see if he was being followed.

Eventually he reached a ramshackle house. It was wedged between two tall factories and served as an opium den and pub—of sorts. He gave a peculiar knock at the door and heard the heavy chain clank as it was unhooked from within. A shadowy figure admitted him and he passed by into a dimly light hallway. The end of the passage was barred by a green curtain that had certainly seen better days. Dragging the tattered cloth aside, he entered what was once a third-rate dancing-saloon. The floor was covered with trampled sawdust and mud mixed with the dark stains of spilled liquor. A sailor was sprawled over an uneven table in the corner and two haggard looking women clung to the rusted bar. The odor of opium hung heavy in the air. An aging staircase at the end of the room led to an obscure, darkened chamber. Standing by the staircase was a disheveled young man with a head of thick blonde hair. He nodded a greeting to Dorian over his thin pipe.

Dorian's voice was low and deep. "That you, Robert? I thought you had left England."

The man sighed heavily as if bearing the weight of the world upon his back. "Nowhere else to go. None of the chaps will speak to me now. I don't really care. As long as I have this stuff, I don't need any friends."

Dorian winced in response and gazed at the other twisted shapes that lay on patched, moldy mattresses in the surrounding rooms. The gaping mouths and listless eyes gave the observer no clue as to what hells or joys they were seeing. Suddenly, he felt the need to be away from this place and particularly away from any other who knew him.

Dorian took one more look at the room before coming to a decision. "I am going on to the other place."

"On the wharf?"

"Yes. The stuff is better there. Come, join me for a drink at the bar before I go."

Robert wearily followed Dorian over to an uneven set of uncomfortable, patchwork-leather stools. The two ordered their drinks from an ugly bartender. He was squat-shaped and bedraggled. His clothes stunk of cheap liquor and piss and he had a long cut over his left eye. The man merely grunted in response and reached behind him, where depressingly dusty bottles waited in a small group. They shared a bottle of French brandy in the stained tumblers the bartender set out on the bar.

The two women sidled up and began demonstrating their wares. When neither of the men showed any interest, the taller one cracked a crooked smile and sneered. "Too proud tonight?"

Dorian's voice was dangerous and threatening. "Don't speak to me. What do you want? Money? Here—now be silent." He slammed coins down on the counter. The woman's eyes flashed for a moment with some hidden retort, before she tossed her unwashed hair and raked the heavy coins from the counter with greedy fingers.

"Good night Robert. Write to me if you need anything."

"Good night then."

As Dorian exited the room and drew the curtain aside, a hideous laugh escaped the painted lips of the woman who had taken his money. She coughed and spoke in a hoarse voice that dripped with venom. "There goes the devil's bargain."

"I told you not to speak!" He glared at the woman and then quickly turned to leave.

Her voice followed his retreat. "Prince Charming indeed.

'Tis what you like to be called, ain't it?"

At those words, the drowsy sailor leapt to his feet as if stung and looked around wildly. He rushed out of the room, hot in pursuit of Dorian.

Dorian moved quickly down the quay, his route was erratic and dictated by any cover that might shield him from the fat drops of rain that fell continuously from the weeping sky. At last he reached a narrow alley that had served him well as a short cut to the next opium den.

As he entered, he was grabbed from behind and slammed brutally against the cold wall. His shoulder stung from the impact. A strong hand that smelled of whiskey and sweat clamped over his mouth to prevent any outcry. Dorian heard the audible click of a revolver, which silenced the yell Dorian was preparing in the back of his throat. The barrel of the handgun was pointed straight at his head. The other side of the weapon was held by a stocky, muscular man. His face was obscured by shadow and a heavy, wool-grey pea jacket.

"Keep quiet," said the man as he removed his meaty palm from Dorian's face. "If you move, I'll shoot you right here on the street."

Dorian gasped as he again inhaled clean air. "Take my wallet—whatever you want."

"I don't want your money. You destroyed the life of my sister, Sibyl Vane. However she died, it was your doing. As soon as I heard the news, I swore an oath to end your life myself. For years I have been tracking you down with nothing but the name she used to call you. You were her Prince Charming. I heard it tonight by happenstance and knew at once that it must be you. At long last, James Vane can take vengeance for his sister. Make your peace with God, Sibyl will be avenged tonight."

Dorian felt the blood drain from him and his fear rose as an ominous storm in the night. His voice sputtered like the rain. "I-I-I d-don't know who you are talking about. You are insane. You have me confused with someone else."

A powerful arm violently pushed Dorian down to the soggy ground. "On your knees and confess your crime! I'll give you one minute to pray, then it all comes to an end."

Dorian panicked, but the gears in his mind began to twirl and spin until he settled on a desperate gambit. "Wait. How long has it been since your sister's death? How many years?"

The man thought for a moment. "Eighteen years. My God has it been that long? But it seems as if only yesterday when I last said goodbye to her. Why does it matter?"

Dorian's forced laugh rang with triumph. "Eighteen years. Look at my face under the lamp."

James paused, then dragged Dorian out and into the street. The light was dim and wavering from the frozen wind and cascading rain, but still it revealed the boyish face of a youth— far too young to belong to the man whom he had sought for all these years. Why, the man he saw before him was nearly the same age as his sister at the time of her death. He had made a terrible mistake. This could not be the same man who had destroyed his sister's life.

James released Dorian and drew back. "My God, I would have murdered you. Forgive me, sir." Aghast at what he had almost done, he turned away quickly and stowed his revolver inside his coat. He moved off, repeating his apologies and asking for forgiveness. Dorian rose slowly to his feet. He trembled as he watched the shadow that had almost ended his life recede into the darkness.

James returned to the place where he had first seen Dorian, immediately ordering and downing two shots of single malt whisky with a shaking hand. The haggard woman who had taken Dorian's money hissed. "Why didn't ya kill him? Ya lummox, he's filthy wi' money an' as vile as they come. Ya wo' have done eve'yone a favor by endin' his miserable life."

"He wasn't who I thought he was. The man I am looking for must be in his forties by now. That one was only a boy."

The woman laughed bitterly. "A bo' ya say? Why, it's been neigh eighteen years sin' Prince Charming turned me 'to what I am."

James growled. "Liar!"

"May God strike me dead here an' now if'n I'm ly'in. He's t'a most vile person I have ever met. They say he sold his soul to the devil, in order to freeze tha' pretty face o' his in time. He has hardly changed in the eighteen years sin' I've met him."

"You swear this?"

"I swear! His real name is Dorian Gray. But ya didn't hear tha' here fro' me. Just keep me away from him. Pe'haps ya could use some company t'night?"

With a disgusted look, he pushed his way free and rushed out into the night. But Dorian Gray had long since disappeared.

CHAPTER 20.

COUNTRY ESTATE

A week later, Dorian was sitting in the conservatory of the country estate of the Duke of Manhound. He had grown paranoid as of late and decided that a change of scenery would be the best thing to rid him of the nagging feeling of being followed. Wherever he went he imagined seeing the haunting face of James Vane in random windows or doorways.

Lady Helena was describing some philosophical treaty, as well as politics and the state of the Stock Exchange. Dorian had difficulty concentrating upon what she was saying. The tea was served with a selection of moist sandwiches and fruity cakes. His thoughts were drawn again to the window and the forest surrounding the estate. Despite the absurdity of it all, he was quite certain that he had seen a shape hiding behind a large oak tree in the distance. A gardener of some sort, certainly. It was only his imagination that Sibyl Vane's brother had followed him out to the country and was now stalking around the trees, waiting for the opportunity to kill him.

In his distracted state he had to be prompted multiple times to respond when the Duke invited Dorian to join his shooting party. They would be hunting for quail. Dorian thought it would make a good distraction and it certainly couldn't hurt to be armed with a gun and cartridges. Shortly thereafter, the two men were afield and striding through the undergrowth engaged in conversation.

Dorian was quite familiar with the Duke and he thought it proper to address him by his first name. "Herbert, how do you find the sport this year?"

"Scarce at best, Dorian. The game is quite sparse this year and I am not sure why. Perhaps the quail have all gone off to the open fields or moved to new ground on the other side of the forest."

"Why would they do that?"

"Surely you have heard of the attacks occurring in the area? It is likely some feral pack of Bulldogs or some sort, but they have frightened away most of the animals. The Duchess has halted her daily rides. She is quite convinced that her prize mare will be set upon and devoured. The servants and gardeners all avoid the woods at night."

Suddenly there was a terrified yell and a single shot rang out from deep within the woods. The trees were suddenly filled with snarling and all manner of disturbing sounds. The head-keeper began shouting and organized the beaters into a group.

The men entered the woods together to search for the source of the commotion. Everyone else in the party was ordered to stay back. After an age, the men emerged dragging a bloody, savaged body between them.

A crowd formed with Sir Beamish at the head. They could see the question on his face as he approached. "What on earth could have killed this man in such a way? If it was a Bull dog he might have hit it. Surely, that shot didn't come from anyone in our line."

Dorian looked on in horror. The head-keeper called a halt to the day's hunt and a groundskeeper ran to notify the local constable. Some poor peasant had met their end in the most gruesome of fashions. The scene filled Dorian with a sense of dread and he decided to pack his things at once. He would take the night-express back into town. He could not spend another night in this accursed place.

Back in his room, Dorian was lying down when a knock came at the door. His valet answered and announced that it was the head-keeper who wished to see him. Dorian frowned. "Please do come in Henderson. Have you come about the terrible accident this morning?"

"Yes, sir."

Dorian picked up his leathered checkbook and jeweled writing pen. "Tell me, was the poor fellow married or had he any dependents? I feel terrible and should like to pay for any necessary arrangements."

"That's the worrisome bit, sir. We don't righ'ly know who he is. T'is why I came to you."

"Whatever do you mean? He isn't one of your men?"

"No, sir. Never seen his face a'fore. Looks ta'me like some sorta' sailor."

The pen dropped from Dorian's hand. "A sailor? Did you say a sailor?"

"Yessir. With both arms tattooed, real rough-like and that sort."

"Was there anything else on him that would give you his name?"

"No sir. He was only carryin' so' money an' a five-shot revolver."

"You must take me to the body at once!"

"Yes sir, if'n you like. He's in an empty stable roun' back. I'll take your Lordship there."

Dorian struggled to mask his apprehension as they walked towards the stables. Upon reaching the door he held up a hand indicating that he would go in alone. The stables were darkened and damp, with a window in the corner providing light enough to see by. The body was wrapped in some sacking in the corner of the stall. Dorian came closer to inspect it. The coarse shirt and blue trousers of the man were ripped to shreds and covered with blood and dirt. Dorian shuddered and looked away from the exposed organs and ragged flesh. Flies buzzed around the corpse and the smell of the voided bowels was nearly unbearable. Determined, Dorian clutched his lace handkerchief to his mouth and pulled away the fabric covering the victim's face. He staggered with relief and a great release of tension rushed from his shoulders. The body was that of James Vane. Tears brimmed in his eyes as he exited the stables, for he knew he was once again safe. The men waiting outside no doubt misinterpreted his crying as tears of sorrow.

CHAPTER 21.

THE SOUL

"Oh, Lady Helena there you are."

"My dear Mr. Gray, you really mustn't shut yourself away like this."

"Tell me what is going on in town? I have not been to the club for ages."

"Everyone is still debating the mysterious disappearance of poor Sage. It is the talk of the town."

"Shouldn't they be tired of that topic by now? They usually tire of such things so quickly."

"Unfortunately, the British public seems quite fascinated with the fate of famous artists and they continue to focus on it. Despite other such news such as Beatrice Ashford's suicide and my own divorce case, they are quite fascinated with Sage's mysterious exodus. Scotland Yard insists she boarded the train to Dover at midnight, the ferry at Calais, and the train to Paris. The French police are adamant that she never even arrived in

185

Paris. Some people have made claims to have seen her leading an artistic revival in San Francisco."

Dorian examined her eyes closely. "What do you think happened to Sage?"

"I haven't the foggiest. Perhaps she is hiding herself away from the world. She may have simply forgotten her plans and ended up painting some great work for months at a time. Or she is dead and I no longer want to think of her. Death is the only thing I have ever been afraid of."

"Why is that?"

Lady Helena paused to light an expensive looking cigarette. "Because, one can survive anything except for death. Now let us take our coffee in the music room—you must play some Chopin for me. My husband ran away with a woman who played Chopin quite exquisitely. Poor man, I was so fond of him and the house is terribly lonely without him."

Dorian stood and together the two walked into the parlor. Lady Helena seated herself in a comfortable leather chair and looked expectantly at Dorian as he seated himself at the piano in the corner. It was a Steinway Grand with rosewood finishes, dark red cabriole legs, and gold edging on the pedal lyre and music rack.

Dorian rested his fingers on the ivory piano keys. Before beginning to play, he looked over warily at Lady Helena. "What if Sage was murdered?"

Lady Helena yawned. "Sage was popular, but terribly dull.

She was not clever enough for enemies. Then again, there are some dangerous places in Paris, but Sage was not likely to visit any of them. She rarely strayed long from her canvas and brushes."

Dorian was quiet for a moment. "What if I told you—that it was I who murdered Sage?"

She laughed in a slow, deliberate way. "It is not possible for you to commit a murder, Mr. Gray. It is something far too vulgar for you and reserved for the lower classes. They take the same pleasure such a beastly act as you and I might in viewing a complex painting. Though, I suppose anything can become pleasurable if one repeats the act too frequently. Let us talk of Sage no longer. It would be highly improbable for her to meet such a romantic end as that. Far more likely that she had too much wine to drink and fell off an omnibus and broke her neck. Someone has simply covered it up out of embarrassment."

Dorian sighed and began playing *Prelude, Op. 28, No. 15*, as Lady Helena strolled across the room. "Besides, her art had suffered much in recent years. I don't think she would have produced the same quality of work as when the two of you were friends. She lost something when the two of you stopped spending time together. Why was it that you became estranged again? I suppose that she bored you. Where did that exquisite portrait she did of you and that wolf pup ever get to? I haven't seen it since it was finished. Now I remember. You said that you had sent it down to the Selby and it was stolen? What a pity. It was quite the masterpiece and I would have loved to buy it to have something to remember dear Sage by."

"How can you speak like that? The whole memory is hateful."

"I don't mean to distress you. I was only wondering. I have been thinking of so many strange things of late. What does it profit someone if they gain the whole world, yet lose their soul?"

Dorian took his hand from the keys and stared at his friend. "Why do you ask me that?"

Lady Helena looked disappointed. "My dear Mr. Gray, I was only curious if you might give me the answer. I have always thought that art had a soul, but mankind clearly does not."

Dorian lowered his head and began to softly play *Mazurkas, Op. 17.* "How wrong you are. The soul is disastrously real. It can be bought and sold, bartered and poisoned like a loaf of bread. I know without a doubt that each of us has a soul."

"How serious you have become. I never thought you would give into the superstitions that plague this world. Do play me something and then tell me as you play, in a lowered voice, how is it you have kept your youth preserved for all of these years? There must be some secret. I am only a decade older than you and I am worn, wrinkled, and faded. But you have never looked more charming or more wonderful. You look just as you did on the first day that I met you. I wish you would tell me your secret. I would do anything to have my youth back. I have so many sorrows that you know nothing of. What an exquisite life you have. The world blossoms at your feet and you have drunk deepest of it all. Yet, for all your experience you are completely unmarred.”

“Don't say that. I am quite changed.”

“No, you are the same. Oh, how I wish I could change places with you. Everyone always has and always will worship you. Your life is your art. You have set yourself and your very being to music and every day is a new sonnet in your world of poetry.”

Dorian stood up and went to the window. He looked out on the full moon hanging in the sky. “There is much you don't know about me as well.”

“Why have you stopped playing? The music was so beautiful tonight—better than you have ever played. If you are tired then I will bid you good night. Tomorrow—we will go tomorrow night to the club.”

“Very well. Good night then.”

Lady Helena rose and paused in the doorway, as if to say something more. Then she merely sighed and walked out.

CHAPTER *22.*

THE PICTURE

As Dorian sat at his walnut Carlton House writing desk, he pondered the many twists and turns of his life. He gazed at the polished ivory knobs and reminisced on how things used to be. How he wished he could go back to how he was in the past. He knew he had corrupted himself with perverse desires and vile fancies. He had done so much evil and been such a terrible influence on others around him. And the awful joy that he took in doing so! He was so ashamed now. Was there no hope for him?

He considered the reflection starring back at him from the golden, carved mirror on the desk. He picked up the hand mirror. It was an antique, inlaid with expensive diamonds and garnets. He studied the face reflected on the polished surface. The bright eyes grew tearful and dimmed despite their beauty. How he loathed his beautiful face. He flung the mirror to the floor and it shattered, with silver splinters flying everywhere. Would that he had been born ugly. Then his life might have been spared the mockery it had become. Youth had spoiled him.

Nothing could change the past. That much was true. It was better not to think of it. He was perfectly safe. No one knew his secret and yet lived. The death of Sage was a perpetual burden that weighed constantly on his mind. More than that though, was his worry over the peril of his soul. Was it trapped in that vile beast that wandered the dark places of the city, senselessly killing animal and human alike? How many times had his childish rivalries, petty revenges, or selfish emotions resulted in the death of an innocent? How many times had someone's death been caused by some unspoken commend of his, to be carried out by that vicious monster? He was responsible for all of it.

Yet, it had been Sage who had painted the portrait and not he. He could never forgive her for that. Everything else had been forced upon him or caused by some temporary madness. All those suicides were their own acts, not forced by his hand. It was nothing to him.

He would start again fresh! He had already begun. Never again would he be tempted to his evil ways. He would be good and kind. If his life became pure, maybe the portrait would change back. Maybe the beast would return to a simple wolf and the killings would stop. Perhaps the portrait had already changed. He would go and look.

Dorian ran and took the winding stairs two-at-a-time.

He quickly unlocked the door and went inside. He approached the tattered screen concealing the portrait with trepidation. Would it have changed already? He stared down at his hands and exhaled slowly. Cautiously, he lifted his hand towards the screen. As he revealed the image behind it, he screamed in outrage. There was no change to the image at all. If anything, it was more loathsome than before. The beast's claws and teeth were covered in a brighter, fresh-looking red blood. The eyes were as malignant as before, but they now seemed to be sadistically mocking him.

He turned away. Should he confess and turn himself in? He laughed at the thought. That was a loathsome idea. Who would even believe his story? There wasn't a single piece of evidence against him to be found. No, he could never confess the truth. There were only two things that could incriminate Dorian Gray—the picture itself and the monster. Why had he allowed either to remain for so long? Perhaps it had been a bizarre curiosity to see how the picture would change and what the wolf would do next. Now the very idea of the creature roaming the streets of London caused him to wake in the middle of the night with chills running down his spine and sweat staining his silk clothes. The painting and the beast were a constant reminder of his guilt. They had served as his conscience. Now they must be destroyed.

Dorian went to the window and opened the large glass pane that overlooked the garden. He flung wide the silk curtains and looked out into the night. With all his mind and concentration he willed the beast to come to his Master—like the pack leader summoning his followers. He spoke one word aloud. "Come."

Turning back to the portrait on the wall, he removed the canvas and set it down on the table. Looking around, he saw a silver Garland knife with an engraved handle that he sometimes used for opening letters. That would have to do. He would slice this work of art that had caused him so much suffering into a hundred pieces. The artist had already been destroyed, so surely destroying the picture would end his torment. Once these reminders of his past was eradicated, then—he would be at peace.

Before he could act, a heavy thud sounded behind him. Dorian turned to once again see the terrifying monster in his room. The giant thing had leapt in through the window and was now in a low crouch. Its terrible muscles rippled with power, ready to be called upon if the need arose. The hands flexed, rising from their lowered position to reveal several inches of razor-sharp claws. They had left deep gouges in the wood of the floor when the creature had landed.

The abomination slowly stood to its full height of nearly three meters. The powerful hindquarters were wolf-like but also like those of a man—but as large as the extremities of an enormous grizzly bear. The pelt of the creature had turned mostly black with tinges of grey along the edges. The jaws and teeth had grown fiercer-looking and more deadly than ever. The snout had reduced in length somewhat, giving a decidedly more human appearance. The large eyes were now a deep blood-red, but were even more intelligent and savage than the last time Dorian had been caught in their gaze.

He tried, unsuccessfully, to hide the shudder that racked his body. He beckoned to the beast with a trembling hand to come to his side. The animal fell down to four legs and approached cautiously, as he had done when still a normal wolf. Dorian was careful to hide the knife, which he gripped with bone-white knuckles, well behind his back. The demon came to rest at his side and looked down in a show of submission. The massive head tilted towards Dorian's hand— inviting a scratch behind the ears as if it were some common dog. After a brief pause, he obliged the request and carefully scratched the spot between the ragged, enlarged ears.

The demon closed its malicious eyes to enjoy the pleasure of a scratch from its master. Dorian carefully raised the knife in his other hand, preparing to strike a downward blow. If done just right, he could puncture the eye and drive the blade deep into the demented brain of the wolf, ending the perverse life.

With all his might, Dorian slashed the knife downward towards his target—and missed, planting the knife deep in the large brow instead. Some keen animal instinct must have alerted the creature of the blow and it had moved, ever so slightly, and avoided the killing blow. Still, blood poured out from the wound and the creature reeled back while letting loose an enraged growl.

The animal flung up the massive claws to paw at the object embedded above its eye. For a moment, the enlarged eyes focused on Dorian and showed a deep and shocked hurt. Then the eyes clouded with a dark, red rage and a terrible howl escaped the throat of the beast. The walls shook with the deep rumble that culminated in a high-pitched blast of sound, nearly inaudible to human ears. It was a howl of challenge for leadership of the pack.

With a roar, the lycanthrope hurled itself furiously at Dorian. Dorian screamed and tried to flee, but he was immediately brought down beneath the bulk of the animal. He was pinned and could do nothing to protect himself as the massive claws slashed wildly and with terrifying speed.

Dorian knew at once that this was to be his end. All his life had been an empty pursuit of pleasure. All the beautiful women he had humiliated and destroyed, the decadent displays of wealth, the many lavish parties, the terrible lies and deceit, the accumulation of so many superficial possessions, and reveling in so many atrocious sins—all of it was now completely empty. Now, at the moment of his death, the memories of his wasted life offered no help or comfort whatsoever.

Blood began gushing from his growing number of

wounds. The massive jaws descended towards the soft skin of his throat. In his final moments, he was left with only regrets over his destroyed friendships and the waste that had been his life. Poor Sage, his dearest friend, would still be alive if they had never met. She had loved him so passionately and he had scorned that love and their friendship as well. How could he have been so cruel to his first love, Sibyl Vane? He realized now that he loved her still and it was only his vanity that had caused him to cast her aside over such a trivial thing. She must have experienced the same choking fear and unrelenting pain as she met her end at the hands of the very same vicious beast.

The wolf clamped down on Dorian's throat and with a mighty wrench of his head ended his Master's life. The beast was suddenly filled with an overwhelming hunger and began devouring the body. The action seemed fitting and cemented his place as the Alpha and pack leader. It was strange, but no other flesh had before tasted as tender and juicy as this. When he had consumed all of the flesh and even the bones, the monster licked the blood clean from the floor. His powerful hunger now sated, he looked out of the great window and saw the full moon in the night sky. With a great howl, he proclaimed his dominance of this territory. Then he surged forward into a run and soared out of the open window, landing once again in the garden below. He sprinted off towards his den in the deep forest. Perhaps he would find some sport to hunt on the way, not for food, but for the thrill of the keenchase and the pleasure of the kill.

II

EPILOGUE

Bright light—beams of painful whiteness penetrated the comfortable darkness and forced Dorian to open his eyes. He was in a thickly wooded area, encircled by a dense wall of trees. He was lying on the mossy ground with his arms flung over the carcass of a half-consumed deer. The forest floor was littered with bones and the air was filled with the foul stench of rotting meat. His skin felt raw and tender. It was completely covered by dried blood and gore. He was utterly naked, like some ghoulish infant at the time of its birth. That was impossible. His last memories were of his gruesome wounds inflicted by the wolf, excruciating pain, and the unpleasant feeling of being eaten alive.

Yet here he was, alive—apparently in the creature's lair. Taking stock of his body, he found he was amazingly uninjured. His hands explored the areas where massive gashes had exposed organs and torn his flesh, but found them all curiously sound and smooth to the touch. Had it all been some terrible dream? Then why was he bloody and in the forest? Whatever had happened, Dorian needed to be away from this place before the lycanthrope returned. Like a newborn fawn on unfamiliar and ungainly legs, he rose and moved falteringly away from the rotting pile of venison. As his legs began to strengthen he stumbled across a small stream and used the water to wash away some of the blood staining his skin. He felt like a common beast as he stooped to slurp up a drink from the muddy water. With his mind somewhat steadied, he focused again on fleeing from the center of the forest in the hope of reaching some safe place.

He ran on, naked skin oblivious to the cuts and scrapes on his feet and arms as he traversed the landscape. He tried following small game trails to make his journey easier. It felt like he ran for hours, dodging amongst the trees. Unbidden, his path led directly to the one location he knew to be both close to the forest and currently uninhabited—Sage's country workshop. With no living relatives, it was unlikely that her recent disappearance would so quickly result in the sale of the property. Dorian approached the estate cautiously. He waited for a time to watch for any signs of life, before dashing to the back door and forcing his way in. The old wooden door seemed to break at the hinges immediately. They must have rotted thin with age.

The hearth was cold and everything remained covered

and put away. The house was just as Sage had left it. He began rummaging through the corner closet. It was good fortune that he found a gentleman's coat that some patron or acquaintance must have forgotten there. Covering his nude and crimson form, he strode into the kitchen and began rummaging through the cabinets. There was an ample selection of cheeses stored in wax, dried fruits, pickled vegetables, salted meat, and even some canned fare. However, none of it appealed. Dorian found that despite his desperate run through the forest, he was still quite full—though from what meal, he had no idea.

He settled on pumping several buckets of water and then scouring his skin clean in Sage's antique, copper tub. He exited the bath and tried not to look at the red-tinted water. With his skin returned to a healthy pink color, Dorian felt once more like himself. And yet, strangely not himself. He was changed and felt like an entirely new version of Dorian Gray. More complete maybe. His mind was swimming with regret, shame, and fear—but also something else. Maybe, there was an inkling of hope there. He felt now that he had the strength to begin a new life. He would gather some meager resources and leave all the wealth and debauchery of his previous life behind him. Perhaps a grand adventure to places unknown in the world, or an excursion to India or the Americas. Any place that took him far away from that demon. It still haunted his vision every time he closed his eyes.

—to be continued soon in: The Wolf of Dorian Gray: Purgatory of the Werewolf

If you enjoyed reading this book, I would appreciate it greatly if you took the time to post a short review on Amazon. Your support makes a tremendous difference. I read each review personally to try and incorporate your feedback into improving the book. Thank you!

ABOUT THE AUTHOR

BRIAN S. FERENCE lives in Cave Creek, Arizona with his wife Rachel and two children Nathan and Lena. He has always had a passion for reading and writing from a young age. Brian loves new experiences, which has included operating his own company, traveling the world, working as a project manager, diving with sharks, and anything creative or fun. He is always up for a new adventure such as writing or other artistic pursuits. You can learn more about book two in The Wolf of Dorian Gray series: Purgatory of the Werewolf at www.thewolfofdoriangray.com or about upcoming books and projects at the author's web site www.brianference.com.

* 9 7 8 0 9 9 8 3 2 5 2 0 0 *